# Close To The Truth

## Shona Husk

## 16pt

**Read How You Want**
LARGE PRINT BOOKS, BRAILLE & DAISY

# Copyright Page from the Original Book

Title: Close to the Truth

Copyright © 2020 by Shona Husk

Published by
Escape
An imprint of Harlequin Enterprises (Australia) Pty Limited (ABN 47 001 180 918), a subsidiary c
HarperCollins Publishers Australia Pty Limited (ABN 36 009 913 517)
Level 13, 201 Elizabeth St
SYDNEY NSW 2000
AUSTRALIA

romance.com.au/escapepublishing/

# TABLE OF CONTENTS

INTRODUCING

# ROMANCE
## .COM.AU

RURAL | CONTEMPORARY | FANTASY | HISTORICAL | PARANORMAL | ROMANTIC SUSPENSE | LGBTQI

All the books you love with all the romance you need!

# Close to the Truth
# Shona Husk

## *Is the truth worth dying for?*

TV biologist, Jasmine Heydon, escaped Bitterwood once. She was 16 and run out of town by the cops for the crime of being born on the wrong side of the tracks. Ten years later, she's changed a lot but Bitterwood hasn't. The town's only claim to fame is the legend of the River Man, a murderous creature who first killed a century ago. Back in town to film a show about the River Man, Jasmine plans to put the mystery to rest once and for all.

Bitterwood's favourite son, Gil Easton, has never forgotten Jasmine, and he's never forgiven his father, the Chief of Police, for running her off. But now Jasmine is back, stirring things up. This time, Gil is determined to stand by her even when the locals want her silenced.

As Gil works to unearth the truth, Jasmine tries to understand her own childhood sighting of the monster. As the threats escalate, the search for the truth grows dangerous ... because the River Man is killing again.

# About the author

**SHONA HUSK** is the author of over forty books that range from sensual to scorching, and cover the contemporary, paranormal, fantasy and sci-fi romance genres. Her most recent series are Face the Music and Coven of the Raven. She lives in Western Australia and when she isn't writing or reading, she loves to cook, cross-stitch and research places she'd one day like to travel.

You can find out more at www.shonahusk.com

www.twitter.com/ShonaHusk

www.facebook.com/shonahusk

Newsletter: https://landing.mailerlite.com/webforms/landing/k5n4n9

# Acknowledgements

Ainslie Paton for always pushing my blurbs to be better.

# Chapter 1

Gilbert Easton smelled the corpse before he saw it. He'd been hunting with his father enough times to know the stink of death and blood. But this wasn't a fresh kill. There was the added sour layer of decay.

'This was reported this morning. I thought you'd want to take a look.' The ranger led the way to the riverbank. An area had been taped off and a young cop was standing guard over the body.

Gil didn't really want to be looking at any bodies, but the committee had nominated him to go because of his police connection, meaning his father.

'Photos would have been fine.' One dead deer three days out from the biggest festival in Bitterwood's calendar, and the only reason tourists came to the town, shouldn't be a problem. The moment the ranger had called the mayor and the mayor had told Gil to get out there, Gil had known why.

This wasn't roadkill or a hunter losing his quarry.

His chest tightened and he glanced at the river. The water was perfectly still. A hundred yards up was where a man had been disembowelled twenty years ago.

Gil knew what he was going to see, and his stomach wasn't ready.

'I'm guessing it was killed yesterday ... probably dusk. That's about right, isn't it?' the cop said.

Gil swallowed and wished he didn't have to breathe. 'Yeah.' He wasn't sure when the River Man made his kills, but it was easier to agree.

'Look, I wouldn't have said anything to the mayor, but there are footprints and the cuts on the body don't look like anything an animal would make.' The ranger lowered his voice. 'It's the River Man, isn't it?'

The ranger, who wasn't a Bitterwood local, seemed almost excited ... or was it worry? Either way there was an edge to his voice and a gleam to his eye that Gil found unsettling.

Gil didn't say anything straight away. He stared at the deer. Its legs were twisted and broken, and the eyes were gone. The crows would have done that.

'The heart missing?' Deer had been turning up dead with their hearts ripped out on a more frequent basis over the last decade. It was a disturbing new turn in the local legend—a legend that was becoming less mythical and more real.

'Ripped clean out,' the ranger agreed. 'Never seen anything like it, except here.' It certainly appeared like a River Man kill. It wouldn't be the first deer, or cow or pig that he'd killed, but it had been twenty years since he'd killed a person.

Gil didn't want to speculate. He was supposed to help shush up anything that would disrupt the festival. 'Maybe it was tourists, hoping to whip up some drama.'

The ranger looked at him like he wanted to ask if Gil had been hit in the head recently. 'If a person did this it's pretty cruel.'

If the River Man did it, then the timing was too perfect. Was he trying to scare people or stir up interest in the festival?

'I think it would be best for everyone if this was quietly cleaned up.

Given the number of people in town, we don't want them traipsing all along the river looking for clues and getting into trouble. We don't need wannabe sleuths.' No, they had professionals coming for that, and they'd want to know all about this.

Jasmine would want to know.

She was coming back.

He hadn't seen or heard anything from her in ten years. Then the mayor had announced that a TV show that specialised in cryptids was coming to Bitterwood for the festival. Gil had watched a few bits out of curiosity and had recognised her in a few seconds.

She was hard to forget. Their parting still made him cringe with residual teenage embarrassment. But she wasn't Jasmine Thorpe anymore. She was Jasmine Heydon. She was someone else's Jasmine now. He may not have forgotten her, but he was sure that he was a distant memory to her. When she'd left town, she hadn't looked back.

He hoped that her coming back wasn't to make the town look dumb on her TV show—not that anyone else had recognised her, so he'd kept that fear to himself. It was his job to make sure that Bitterwood came out looking good and that more people wanted to come to the festival next year. The mayor saw the TV show as free promo.

Gil pulled out his smartphone and took some pictures of the deer and the footprints that led back into the river. This would be all the TV show got. Bitterwood didn't need people coming in and telling them it was all a hoax when they'd lived with the mysterious deaths for a century.

He shivered. Hoaxes didn't last for over a hundred years. Even though he'd been born and raised in Bitterwood, he couldn't quite believe that there was a creature that lived around the river eating the occasional heart. He glanced at the deer. The deer would probably disagree with him.

'That's it? Just dispose of it?' The ranger's eyebrows lifted.

Gil sighed. 'What do you want to do? Full forensic testing? Question everyone in town? It's a deer. Plenty get hunted and no one bats an eye.'

'Hunters use bullets.' The ranger jerked his chin at the young cop. 'What about you? You're the cop. What are we looking for?'

'Um.' The young man's voice wavered. He looked at the river, then the deer and then the scrub behind him that gave way to forest. He looked like he was straight out of high school and still terrified of the local legend. 'I think ... I mean it looks like the River Man's work.'

'There you go; the cops are on to it. They'll hunt down the River Man and put him in the zoo.' Gil forced a smile. The cops would do nothing. There wasn't anything they could do, and they wouldn't be wasting limited resources on a deer when there were hundreds of extra people in town.

The ranger crossed his arms. 'So we'll pretend this didn't happen, just like the last one. Don't want to spoil the party.'

'That's pretty much what I was told.' Gil shrugged. He didn't like it either. They should be gathering evidence. Maybe if they did, they'd eventually have something. But what?

# Chapter 2

Jasmine read the list in front of her. Batsquatch, pterosaurs and the River Man. She had three weeks in Washington State tracking down the local legends. There was nothing ordinary about her job as the biologist on the television show *Cryptid or Hoax*? She read the list of cryptids again and tried to ignore the flutter of fear the River Man caused.

It was a hoax. It had to be. There was no such thing as amphibious humanoids.

Logically she knew that, but her six-year-old self who'd seen it fighting with her uncle wasn't convinced. She was sure that a psychologist would say she'd taken this job to soothe her inner child. The reality was being a TV zoologist paid better than anything else she'd found, and she needed the money to pay off her giant student loans. She owed more money than her parents had ever earned.

And now she was going to have to see those parents for the first time in ten years. It would be hard to avoid them, given that the River Man hung around Bitterwood. She doubted its population of five thousand had grown while she'd been away. She glanced at Luke Melrose, who researched the local lore, and the host Calvin LeRoux, who could make anything sound interesting. As colleagues and travel buddies they were great, but they also thought she was from Seattle. No one knew that she was a backwater Bitterwood brat so far from the right side of the track that she couldn't even see the train.

Now probably wasn't a good time to start sharing. No one liked an over-sharer.

'We'll be there for the River Man Festival,' she said, trying to sound enthused. If that wasn't an excuse to listen to bad local music and get drunk, nothing was. When she'd lived there, even being underage hadn't stopped her. If she hadn't been caught with her hands all over the local Chief of Police's son ten years ago, she might still be living in Bitterwood doing exactly that this weekend.

Gilbert Easton was the other reason she didn't want to go to Bitterwood. He was unfinished business—quiet literally as she'd been hauled half naked out of the car and told to get out of town. She wasn't stupid, so she took the chief's fifty-dollar note and took off like the devil was on her tail, only stopping when she landed on her aunt's doorstep in Seattle. Fortunately, her father's side of the family was a touch more respectable and her aunt hadn't thrown her out.

She really owed the chief a thank you.

She wasn't sure what she owed Gil—possibly that BJ she never got to finish. She bit back a grin. He was probably married to some local girl from the right family who didn't know how much he liked to get his hands dirty. He'd always been the town's favourite son and she'd always wanted to knock his halo off.

'Think of the interviews. The potential eye witnesses.' Calvin loved the local angle ... especially if it was female and wanted to love him back.

Jasmine smiled. He had no idea what Bitterwood was like.

Luke walked over with the keys to the rental SUV in his hand. 'Got our ride. Ready?'

Nope. But she never would be. Bitterwood was the last place she wanted to go. She'd rather visit the Arctic to do a special on Santa Claus. Hell, she'd rather analyse scat for bone fragments to determine what the local wolf population was eating.

She smiled. 'Can't wait.' *Kill me now.*

'How are you going to dress this one up in a lab coat?' Luke nudged her. He definitely had the easy job.

'There must be old photos from the crime scenes ... claw marks, footprints and tracks. I can talk for hours.' She made each word slower. 'He has kills going back a century. Not scared, are you?'

Her heart beat faster, reminding her that she was afraid. She'd seen it. It had been dusk and she'd been playing hide and seek with her brother and cousin. They hadn't found her—she'd thought it was because she was good at hiding, turned out at ten they were just real good at getting into her uncle's weed—she'd wished they would find her as the monster appeared. She'd squeezed her eyes shut and stayed there until it was dark. By the time she opened her eyes, the monster and her uncle were gone, the field near the river was empty except for a few stranded car bodies that had been there for as long as she could remember. She'd run home expecting to tell her tale, but her uncle was talking to her mother as though nothing had happened and she'd stayed silent.

Luke shook his head. 'Myths don't kill.'

'Cryptids do.' Calvin's eyes narrowed as he thought about the possibilities. 'This could be legit.'

'Nope. It has to be a hoax.' A hoax was something man-made to draw attention and trick people. A myth, on the other hand, had no real substance, just some sightings and a place in the collective consciousness. A cryptid was something that couldn't be explained. It had one foot in myth and another in reality. Sometimes they came across stuff that could be based on fact ... but the story grew bigger than the actual creature. Much like when guys went fishing and the size of the catch went up with every beer and retelling.

There was no way the River Man was real. She refused to believe that. Science wouldn't let her believe that.

'A hundred-year-old hoax? Nah, back then they believed in the boogie man,' Calvin said. 'Would've started with some feud and someone not wanting a murder charge.'

'His last murder was twenty years ago.' Every so often the River Man would kill a human instead of a deer. Most of the mysterious creatures they investigated had allegedly killed at least once. They didn't keep coming back. The River Man was an anomaly. Maybe it was a giant lizard? A family of alligators?

She didn't want to go to Bitterwood and find out the truth.

'Cool, that means there will be people alive who remember it.' Calvin was looking far too happy.

He'd probably be thrilled to know that she was one of those people. It was going to be best to keep her mouth shut and hope that no one in Bitterwood recognised her. They probably all thought she was dead.

A few hours later, they reached the orchards that marked the edge of town. It was such a familiar sight. Her throat closed for a moment as they went over the bridge. She looked left toward what had been a popular spot to park as teenagers—it was now a picnic area.

Not much else in town seemed to have changed. Maybe there were a few new buildings. They drew in closer to the town centre, past the primary school and one of the churches. The fire station. It was all so familiar and so small. After living in Seattle and travelling all over the States in search of the weird and wonderful, Bitterwood seemed so ... dull. She couldn't believe that once she'd thought the town was everything, and that she'd never belong anywhere because she couldn't belong here.

Calvin parked the SUV out the front of the motel. It was the good motel, she noted with a small measure of relief. Or it had been the good motel, maybe it wasn't anymore. Unlike her aunt she'd never come back, not even for Christmas, even though she knew her mother would want to see her. She'd always been worried that if she came back, she wouldn't be able to get free again. If it wasn't for work, she wouldn't be coming back now.

Her stomach tightened and she wished she hadn't had that greasy double bacon with extra cheese burger for lunch, or the large coffee to wash it down with. There was no way she was going to be able to avoid running into people that she knew. No, but she could pretend not to know them.

After ten years, she didn't know them.

And they didn't know her.

She wasn't the same person she'd been when she'd lived here, but she knew that wouldn't stop them from thinking that they knew her. Her aunt was still that kid who ran away to join the Navy, abandoning her family and leaving her mother to look after four younger children—like it was somehow Tricia's responsibility as the eldest to be the second mother to them. Over forty years since she'd left and her aunt still wasn't forgiven.

Jasmine sighed and undid her seatbelt. 'I'll check us in, if you bring in the stuff.'

It was the usual deal. This time she was reluctant to leave the safety of the SUV, but the guys would notice if she started acting weird, so she had to get on with it. She got out of the SUV, pulled a face at them and raised her hands in claws. They did the same.

This job was so much better than working in a lab.

She turned away from the vehicle and drew in a deep breath. The air was damp from the river and there was the scent of the orchards that surrounded the town. Did her brother still work at the cannery? Was her mom still a cleaner at the school? She doubted her dad was doing much more than he used to, which was very little. He'd done odd jobs and helped her uncle out a few times. Her parents had argued about that. There was some kind of rift between Mom and her brother.

Families. They were way more drama than she needed. It would be at least another ten years before she came back again.

With her back straight, she walked into the motel. She spent half her life on the road and these days they all tended to look the same. It was only the very bad or very good that stood out. This was neither. It was beige and bland. Vending machine to one side, a few tourism brochures and a poster about the River Man Festival. She paused to look at it. There was a sketch of the monster, details of the bands that would be playing, cake stalls, a performance by the high school and a friendly game of baseball between the fire and police departments. It was now a three-day festival. It had grown while she'd been gone.

'You here to see the River Man?'

The man's voice made her jump. She turned around and fixed a smile, she didn't recognise him. *Good start.* 'Yep.'

*God I hope not.*

He nodded. 'This year is extra special. I think he knows about our festival.'

'Really?' Was the River Man going to walk into town and sign autographs? Had people stopped fearing him? She couldn't imagine the town changing that much.

'Mutilated deer was found near where that hunter Jim ... Jimmy Nebbit was killed. That must be a couple of decades ago. His mom just passed.'

She fought to keep her smile fixed and look curious, not terrified. The River Man was still actively killing.

'Yeah,' the man kept going. 'No one is saying it's the River Man, most people don't even know it happened, but I have a police scanner. Comes in handy. But it's the kind of thing he does.'

'Kill deer?' She forced the words out.

He nodded. 'There's been a deer found every few years. Only ever takes the heart.' He gave Jasmine a conspiratorial wink.

That sounded like the River Man was a more active killer than he'd been when she'd lived here. Back then it had been the occasional human killed, and by occasional she meant there would be decades without anything more than a sighting.

'Happy to give you the latest on the River Man, grab a flyer on the festival, but you'll have to camp out as there are no free rooms in town.'

'Got a reservation.' She gave the network's details.

His eyebrows lifted and he peered a little closer at her as though trying to work out if he should know her. She'd changed her surname when she'd turned eighteen, opened up the phone book and taken a stab ... several stabs because she hadn't liked the first three. 'You're that TV scientist.'

Oh great, they got cable and watched her show. She kept her smile in place and released a tiny sigh of relief. No, not her show, a show.

'I checked out a few clips on the internet after you lot booked.' He looked pleased with himself. 'First time someone close to famous has stayed here.'

There was a reason for that. No one came to Bitterwood for fun. There was some fishing, some hiking and the festival. That was it.

The man handed over the room keys. Luke and Cal shared, and she usually shared with the boom operator who was also female. It wouldn't have bothered her to share with a guy, but it bothered others. She was pretty sure she didn't have girl cooties.

'We'll be around for the rest of the week. Hoping to get some interviews from people who've seen him.' She jerked her head in the direction of the poster.

'There'll be some of them all right. Although if you ask me, most of the sightings were after too many beers.' He gave her another wink.

Jasmine was hoping that there was something wrong with his eye. Maybe he did recognise her and her reputation had survived her absence? 'We know how to weed them out.'

Calvin and Luke joined her, carrying all the luggage. They didn't believe in making second trips. The man gave directions and they made the short trip across the car park to their rooms. She dumped her stuff in her room. Tonight she'd have it to herself. The rest of the crew wouldn't get here until the day after tomorrow and there were things to film.

Then she went and knocked on the guys' door so they could get started. There was a lot of prep work to get done this afternoon. They weren't getting paid to sit around. Once on location, they had to hit the ground. These days they had a system happening. The door swung open, like her they hadn't even bothered to open their cases.

'So I set up a meeting with the festival committee for this evening. Mayor will be there so make nice with him.' Calvin smiled. He'd set up most of the meetings ahead of time. 'One of the committee members will take us to the locations of the sightings.' He glanced at her. 'They didn't mention any murders.'

'Did they mention a very recent mutilated deer that fit the creature's MO?'

Both men looked at her. 'What?'

'That would be a no then?' She gave them a quick update on the latest gossip. Of course the committee and mayor weren't going to be spruiking about the River Man's kills—that might scare people away.

'If this classy website is to believed, there have been six murders, don't know how many deer.' Luke had his laptop open. *Monster Deaths* was a website they had stumbled across more than once. Sometimes it tallied with what they discovered, sometimes it was as wild as the goose they were chasing. This time it was accurate. Bitterwood locals kept tallies. They probably knew exactly how many deer had been found over the years.

What troubled her was that only the heart was taken. An animal would eat more than that. Then there was the random nature of the kills; animals needed to eat regularly, which meant either there were a whole lot of deer that hadn't been found or it wasn't an animal they were dealing with.

Calvin swore and shook his head. 'I wanted to be a newsreader, not following up on dead deer.'

'The deer will give us something to talk about, and if there's a murder this weekend you'll get to play reporter too.' Jasmine beamed at him even though a shiver ran down her spine. Her uncle had survived fighting with the monster. But she couldn't remember any other River Man assaults, only kills. Time to change the topic. 'So who's on the festival committee, any vested interests?'

'Pfft. They're on the committee.' Luke shrugged. 'In a town this small there'll be plenty of conflicts of interest.'

'You know what I mean.' Some places didn't really want their monster investigated even though they said they did.

'They want the River Man looked into, but I got the impression they also want some fluff on the festival,' Calvin said as he handed out some info on the town.

'That's a given. But it shouldn't be hard to work that into the interviews?' She glanced at Calvin. He just nodded. 'With luck I'll be able to get fresh samples or footprint castings ... maybe even see the deer.' She paused while the guys smirked. 'But I can talk about possible creatures he could be, and also the biology of an amphibian?'

'Yeah, once I get into the local lore we should be able to spin up something. I wonder if it goes back more than a century?'

'You thinking First Nation?' Calvin made some notes.

'I'll look into it. Ask the committee. Some of these creatures have been around for a while. Remember Champ of Lake Champlain?'

They all nodded. No proof he existed and yet he'd persisted for centuries. They had concluded that he wasn't a hoax or cryptid, but probably a sturgeon fish. They had then received a bunch of emails from people who'd seen it. Some hadn't been very nice about getting their point across.

Every so often they came across something they couldn't explain and they called it a cryptid. She suspected that this episode would fall into that basket. It was always good to have a balance of results.

Jasmine leafed through Calvin's hand-out. She was curious about what he'd included, and more importantly, who was on the festival committee. There was a map with a few River Man sightings marked on it, plus where to find the festival activities.

She glanced at him. 'Did you pull this off the town website?'

'They sent it to me. There's a brief bio of the committee members too as they thought we might find that useful. At the end.' Calvin flipped her papers.

One name jumped out at her.

Gilbert Easton.

She struggled to focus on the page so she could read his bio. All two lines of it. Owner of Easton's Hardware and volunteer firefighter. Family has been in Bitterwood for generations.

It sure had, Easton's Hardware was on Easton Road.

Of course he was going to be on the committee. That was exactly the kind of thing he did. He was so much a part of the community, they were symbiotic organisms and they'd die if separated. Even at school he'd been involved in everything. She'd tried once but had quickly discovered that not everyone was welcome. After that she'd given up on fitting in and had done her best to be difficult.

Jasmine didn't remember going after Gil, but somehow they had gotten together for a few weeks ... it might have even lasted the whole summer if his father hadn't intervened. Or it might have ended once he grew tired of slumming and paying for every movie.

'So, who's our guide going to be?' She hoped her voice sounded casual.

'Gilbert Easton, he's the Chief of Police's son.' Calvin smiled. 'Guess we'd better be on our best behaviour.'

That wouldn't matter as Gil only knew her at her worst.

# Chapter 3

Gil drummed his fingers on the table in the meeting room in the council offices. It was just past five. He was early. He'd shut the store that had once been his grandfather's a few minutes before five to make sure he got here early.

Hoping to catch sight of Jasmine before the meeting?

Or just trying to get it over with as fast as possible?

He wasn't sure. He'd tried to find out where she'd gone when she'd left, but no one had known. She'd just hitched a ride out of Bitterwood and vanished. She'd never even called him to say she was alive. Part of him wasn't surprised. After what his father had done, Gil had refused to speak to the man.

Her leaving wasn't a shock, even though the timing was. He'd always known that she had no roots and no reason to stay. Maybe that had been part of the attraction—unlike some of the girls who were from local and respectable families, she hadn't wanted anything more than a good time. She had never tried to sink her claws in. He was still fighting off some of those same girls, now women, who thought it was time he settled down.

While at times he wanted to leave, nowhere else would ever be home. Easton blood had built this town. And now he owned part of it. He couldn't up stakes and leave. But he'd be damned if he'd marry because it was the right thing, or about time. While he loved the town, his life was not going to be ruled by the committee of busybodies who thought they knew best.

Tap. Tap. Tap. His fingers never broke their rhythm.

The mayor had been keen to get *Cryptid or Hoax?* in. Gil hadn't been so convinced. The town could come out looking gullible, or worse, the River Man could end up looking like a money-generating gimmick. So he'd researched the show and had nearly choked on his beer when he'd seen her. He'd had to check that it was her and not someone who looked like Jasmine Thorpe.

It was her. All grown up and with a masters in zoology.

And a change in surname. She was probably married.

The girl voted most likely to spend her eighteenth birthday in jail had performed a miracle on herself. While he was as dumb as the boxes of hammers he sold. After falling out with his father, he'd refused to join the police force and had instead agreed to take over the shop from his grandfather. He'd done some online studies about bookkeeping and running a business, even set up online ordering for the farmers so they didn't have to drive in.

'Gil.' The mayor clapped a hand on Gil's shoulder as he walked past. 'Not putting yourself forward to be a councillor?'

'No, sir, got too much else to do.' He was going to leave that for the folks with twenty years on him. He still wasn't sure how he'd got roped into being on this committee. Guess someone had to do it and if everyone chipped in there was less work to go around.

The other committee members bustled in. Nancy who'd been acting as secretary for over thirty years, the bar owner Greg and a couple of other store owners ... geez, it looked as though the festival committee was made up of proprietors looking for a quick tourist buck.

He knew that wasn't true; the River Man was local legend and the festival had started out as a glorified market day and a chance to remember the victims. Would Jasmine defend the place she'd grown up in or throw Bitterwood under the bus, the way it had done to her?

Gil had no idea. They'd been kids who hadn't spent a vast amount of time talking.

Talking and footsteps made his fingers still. Nancy glanced at him. Did they all remember her and what had happened? The urge to fidget made his leg jump, but otherwise he kept his discomfort safely suppressed. He didn't like being the focus of attention.

Jasmine had, but it had always been for the wrong reasons.

Two men and a woman entered the meeting room. They all held take-out coffees—did they think the council's wouldn't be up to scratch? And they all wore cargo pants and shirts with the TV show logo on. Subtle.

He tried to give all three a casual once-over but his gaze snapped back to Jasmine. Her blonde hair was pulled back in a loose knot, her outgrown bangs swept the side of her face. There was no dyed chunk of hot pink or whatever colour was her new favourite and no red lipstick. Her make-up was so careful it almost looked as though she wasn't wearing any.

She looked polished and professional. He realised then that he didn't know Jasmine Heydon at all and that Jasmine Thorpe was long gone. And from the polite, yet fixed smile on her lips, she didn't appear to recognise him either.

The mayor did the introductions as the three sat.

They wanted access to archives and the local history centre, if there was one. Names of people who'd seen the River Man. Gil listened. Her voice was the same, but with no swearing punctuating her sentences. The whole time she avoided looking at him and kept on acting as though she didn't know anyone in the room.

That was bullshit.

The mayor had been their math teacher. Nancy's grandkids had been a year below them at school. He'd known most of the people in the room, enough to recognise and say hi, his whole life.

'Gil has volunteered to spend his day off to take you to the sighting locations. Farmers trust him on their land.' The mayor smiled as though everything was peachy. What was implied was that they weren't welcome to go gallivanting all over the town on their own.

Gil wished he'd never volunteered but he'd thought the best way to keep an eye on the TV show was to be super helpful. If he'd known Jasmine was involved, he'd have never volunteered. Protecting the town was coming back to bite him on the ass already.

All eyes turned to him. Including hers. There was a flicker of something before she lowered her gaze to her coffee and took a sip.

'Yeah, I'll pick you up at eight am, there's a bit of ground to cover if you want to go all the way back to the first sightings.'

'And the most recent.' Jasmine smiled.

Did she know about the deer? Gil glanced at the mayor who had paled and was struggling to find some words.

Gil gave a reluctant nod. If they already knew, there was no harm.

'And I'd like to see the carcass and any photos.' Another smile that was cool and professional. She knew all about the deer.

The mayor coughed. 'That won't be possible. It's already been destroyed. Health hazard. Gil will take you to the site though.'

'Yes, and I'd like to see any old maps you have to from around the time the River Man first appeared. I'd love to know how the story started. Do you know if there's any First Nation legends?' the younger man, Luke, said. He was the one who researched the local lore, making the show a bit of myth and a bit of biology.

'You'd be best heading up to Colville Reservation,' Nancy said.

Luke looked at his co-workers. 'I might skip the tour and take the SUV.'

Now if Gil could get rid of the other man, he'd have Jasmine to himself and he'd be able to ask why she'd never picked up a phone. He'd thought she was dead. For a while the kids had started a rumour that the River Man had taken her.

That was probably better than word getting around about what had really happened. Not that his father would have ever admitted to yanking her out of the car half naked—and Gil in much the same state—and threatening her with jail for underage drinking and a whole pile of other charges that would have never held up.

That hadn't mattered though. The words that had cut had been personal. His father had threatened her family. Gil had never forgotten. 'If I ever catch you with my son again I will make sure your family pays.'

Gil had argued with his father as he'd done up his pants.

His father had claimed that she was just looking to get pregnant and get married. Then he'd pulled out the old *not while you're living in my house* routine.

The next day Gil had moved in with his grandfather, above the shop.

Jasmine had already left town. It had been a kick to the nuts. People telling him that she was a tramp and had done him a favour hadn't helped. He knew she'd been nicknamed Jezebel. He knew he wasn't her first, but she'd been his. He hadn't cared what people thought of her. He'd known her and she'd have never done anything to put her family at risk.

He still didn't care what they all thought of her. When he looked at her across the table that spark of desire reignited in his blood. She was all but ignoring him, acting as though they'd never met. But it was an act, because he'd noticed when she'd snuck glances at him. And only him.

His gaze lowered to her left hand. No sign of any rings, not even a tan line. Divorced? He wanted to know what had happened to her in the last ten years. Even if it was just a catch-up over coffee. He almost believed that lie, then her gaze met his.

'This is already sounding like a cryptid because of its longevity.' She smiled and he recognised that look. All trouble, and when it turned on him, all seduction. There was a glimmer in her eyes she couldn't quite hide. 'I can't wait to get to the bottom of this mystery.'

Neither could he. Because as much as he'd tried not to think about her over the years, the not knowing had been a scab that he'd go back and pick just to see if it still hurt.

It did.

She'd been his first lust. They'd never had a chance to become more. Seeing her now though, he knew if she'd stayed for him she'd have been trapped, her wings clipped.

He wanted to watch her fly and get to know her again.

Which either made him a masochist or desperate, as she'd flit away as soon as she was done. He wasn't sure that they were done.

***

It was with gritted teeth that Gil picked up Jasmine and the TV show's host Calvin. Jasmine had left the meeting last night without a backward glance, but he hadn't gone after her either. Now they would be stuck in his truck with a chaperone for the day. Considering their track record with cars, a chaperone was probably a good idea.

And if Jasmine was acting as though she didn't know him, he could return the favour.

'Hope you're ready to do some walking.' He took a quick glance at their footwear, but both presenters had sensible hiking boots on. They also had daypacks. Did they think he planned to ditch them in the mountains?

Jasmine sat in the back seat. She immediately started looking at the map as if she was unfamiliar with the area. Gil bit his tongue. If she was pretending to be a stranger here, there was a reason, but he wanted to know why.

He drove out of town.

'I thought we'd start at the furthest point and work our way back, unless you want to go in chronological order?'

Gil met Jasmine's gaze in the rear-view mirror.

'Too much time between kills for the chronological order to be relevant. The spread is interesting though. The older murders attributed to the River Man seem to be further up the Columbia.' She glanced at the map again.

'Climate change forcing him south?' Calvin said with a smirk.

Gil ignored him. 'There have been animal kills attributed to him further north.'

'Confirmed? Are there ranger reports? Sightings?' She leaned forward as if interested and Gil couldn't help but grin.

'Can't say for sure. Besides, you guys get paid the big bucks to do the research.' All the committee had done was pull together what was easy to find. Most locals knew where the River Man had killed people and animals. Although he wouldn't put any money on it all being the River Man—he wasn't even sure he believed in the town legend.

'First stop will be the deer site from a few days ago. Might as well see what's left.' He turned into a dirt driveway and kept going until they reached the fence and had to walk to the river.

There was a little tape still clinging to the tree. Any tracks the River Man had made had been trampled over when the carcass had been removed. There wasn't much to see.

Jasmine pressed her lips together. 'They made a mess of this. Would have been smarter to preserve the site and carcass for us. It could've given us some valuable information.' She looked at him. 'It's almost like someone didn't want us to learn too much.'

She knew who he was, but she was never going to admit it in front of anyone. Did she not want her co-workers to learn too much about her and her past? Or did she not want Bitterwood to learn about her? He wanted to reassure her that no one would care, but he couldn't be sure that it wouldn't be a lie.

Calvin gave her an unsubtle nudge. The spell was broken when she glanced at her colleague.

'The mayor thought it best not to draw attention. Didn't want to worry the festival goers.' And didn't want the town to miss out on the tourist dollars.

'Couldn't put the carcass in the freezer? I'm sure there'd be someone around here with a freezer big enough,' she pressed.

She knew damn well there would be. There were plenty of hunting families.

'You'll have to take that up with the mayor, but he's very busy.' The mayor didn't want to answer any questions, only get his five minutes in front of the camera. 'I took some photos. I can print them out if you'd like, or email them?'

'Email would be great.' She handed him her business card.

That had been far too easy. Now he had her email and number and she didn't seem the slightest bit concerned. Her smile became one that he recognised, but was gone just as fast.

'So that man was murdered not far from here?' She pointed up the river as if she'd never been there before.

Most teenagers had been dared to go there at least once.

'Sure, but there's nothing to see there now.'

They spent the rest of the morning traipsing along the riverbanks or through farmers' fields.

He hadn't lied. There really wasn't much to see and certainly no fresh evidence. He doubted very much that the river and land had remained the same over the course of a century. As they made their way back to the car after the final stop, Calvin started to lag behind.

'He doesn't really like being outside, does he?' Gil said as he moved closer to Jasmine.

She glanced at him, but didn't pull away. 'No. There's too much nature. He much prefers people to animals.'

'What about you?' *Talk to me Jasmine. You know me.*

'I have a masters in zoology, take a guess.' That glint was in her eyes again. 'Animals don't lie. They treat each other better than people often treat each other ... except dolphins. Dolphins are dicks.'

'I don't believe that. Aren't they meant to be smart?'

She nodded. 'But they act like drunken frat boys after a bit of ass.'

That was more like the Jasmine he knew. 'It's good to see you again, Jasmine.'

Her back stiffened and the smile was gone. In that second a shadow flicked over her face, before the polite and distant smile reattached itself to her lips. 'I'm not that person anymore.'

'I can see.' That wasn't a bad thing ... but she didn't seem real happy either. They reached the car in silence. Calvin was about fifty yards back. Had he seen them talking and dropped back even further?

'Are you going to tell everyone?' She shoved her hands into her pockets. Her gaze firmly on her co-worker, not him.

'Nope. Not my place to tell everyone.' Plenty wouldn't be happy to see she'd come back successful. 'I would like to know what happened though. You never said goodbye.'

She snorted and lifted an eyebrow. 'That what you really thinking?'

The back of Gil's neck heated and it crept up his throat before hitting his cheeks. 'We had more than that.'

'Did we? That night is pretty well burned into my brain.'

'Yeah, mine too.' And for all the wrong reasons. 'I wondered what had happened to you.' He hadn't forgotten her. She'd been the first girl he'd been with. She'd been hard to forget.

'And now you know.' She glanced at him and tilted her chin, as if daring him to argue.

He dared. He wasn't going let this chance slide by, not now that she'd admitting to remembering him. 'Get a drink with me tonight.'

'And start the gossip mill turning?'

'I'm the one who lives here, you can leave.' There was nothing the town gossips could say that he hadn't heard the first time around.

'Fine. Let's call it work.'

If that's what it took. 'I'll bring those photos and some other bits.'

'Blank paper?' She teased.

He shook his head. 'I don't want Bitterwood to look bad. I'm here to help.'

She laughed. 'Some things never change.'

Calvin made it back to the car. He put his hands on his hips. 'How many bits of mud do we need to look at?'

'It's called habitat. I'm looking for similarities, and also evidence that the River Man exists. Footprints, meal leftovers, a nest. Anything.' She walked around and opened up the car door.

This Jasmine was all about work. Things did change, but he could see the younger Jasmine in there. She still had attitude and wasn't afraid to speak up. These days people listened to her.

'Good news is the owner of the next farm saw the River Man.' Gil wouldn't mind leaving the man with the farmer so he got a bit more time with Jasmine. 'I'll give him a call and see if he wants to chat.'

Calvin gave a fist pump. 'That would be great. You two can stare at the mud.'

\*\*\*

Jasmine watched the river. This was the scene of the River Man's first human kill according to the town lore.

There would be old police records or newspaper clippings to confirm it. Had he been murdered the same way, or had the MO changed over the years? She needed to know. The most recent man had had his throat slashed and he'd been covered in cuts—his heart had been torn out. It had been summer. She remembered the day as it had been around the time she'd seen the River Man.

Standing here was enough to make her shiver, as if old, restless ghosts were rising out of the water.

Gil moved closer. 'Do you think he's real?'

The River Man had been a hot topic at school. No one had said much about the victim. She was sure that it would be easy to find out a little more about all of the deaths, however she wasn't here to investigate murders.

She was here to look for the creature and give some theories about what it could be. She had no idea.

'I don't know. It shouldn't be ... and yet ... this doesn't fit typical hoax patterns. And myths tend to have historical deaths, not recent ones.' She shrugged and glanced upriver, round the bend and up a ways was her uncle's property. The image of him fighting with the monster flashed in her mind. It could've easily been him. Plenty would have said good riddance if he'd been killed. 'How many deer have been found?'

'Since you left? Four.'

'That's more than I remember for the sixteen years I lived here. Maybe the River Man now has a family to feed.'

Gil gave a snort of laughter as he scuffed his boot in the weeds at the edge. 'You could make us look like a bunch of inbred morons.'

She laughed and shook her head. 'It wasn't my idea to come here. But as with every episode, we do our best to put together something interesting. A bit of local lore, some facts. It's entertainment with a touch of science.'

'You make it respectable.' He flashed her a smile.

No one had ever accused her of making anything respectable. Her lips curved. Even after ten years he still had the power to lift her mood and make her smile.

'Thank you for showing us around.' She turned and started toward the car. Her camera full of photos and her notebook full of scribbles about what she'd seen. None of it was as helpful as seeing the actual deer would have been.

'You didn't need me.'

No she didn't. But that didn't mean that she didn't want him. Being alone with him made it easy to slip back into old habits. 'Your wife won't mind you meeting me for a drink?'

That was blatant fishing, but she didn't care. She didn't want to be seen with him if he had someone waiting at home. She wasn't going to be that woman.

'Not married.'

'Girlfriend?' She lifted an eyebrow.

'None of them either.' He smiled as though he'd been waiting for her to return—that or she was imagining he was still interested. There'd only been one reason boys had been interested in her back then and it had been the same reason she'd been interested in them.

'That I find hard to believe. You must be one of the most eligible bachelors in town.' She'd thought he'd be married, yet here they were planning drinks as if nothing had changed. It was weird.

She hated Bitterwood and her whole life here. But she didn't hate Gil, never had. His father, on the other hand ... and his father was still Chief of Police.

He grunted and nodded. 'No one ever left an impression the way you did.'

That hadn't always been a good thing. 'I did exit in a rather spectacular way.'

'How about you? Married?'

'No.' She shook her head.

'It didn't work out?'

'I changed my name because I wanted to, not because of some guy.' It had seemed like the right thing to do. The final nail in Jasmine Thorpe's coffin. 'Maybe meeting up for a drink isn't a great idea. I'm not here to pick up where I left off, Gil.'

'I thought we decided it was a business meeting?' He grinned as though he was completely innocent of anything she could possibly accuse him of. That was the trouble with Gil, he always came out of every scrape with his halo firmly in place. Not even getting caught with her had dented it.

'Your dad won't be happy when he realises I'm back.' She didn't want anyone realising that she was back. If she started hanging around with Gil, people might notice. Of course they would notice. Gossip would be all over town before they'd finished their first beer—but would they think she was the old Jasmine returned?

'I don't care.' Something hardened in his eyes for just a moment. What had happened after she left? 'Besides, aren't you going to see your folks while you're here?'

She knew she should, but she really didn't want to. She shrugged. She probably would, because if her mother found out she'd been back and not seen her she'd be devastated. Jasmine couldn't do that to her mother.

'Your mom used to ask if I'd heard anything from you.'

'I'm sure my aunt passed on information.' What was said Jasmine didn't know, as her aunt had refused to be a go-between.

If Jasmine had stayed, Gil's father would've made sure that her family suffered. Sure they were probably breaking a few little laws, but a vendetta against her shouldn't be extended to her family. The Chief of Police should know better than to use his position to make other people's lives hell; she wished she'd known that ten years ago.

Gil placed a hand on the hood of his truck, he looked over at her and smiled. 'I missed having you around. You always made things interesting.'

'Is that why you dated me?' If what they did could be called dating ... a couple of burgers and some make-out sessions. 'I thought you just wanted to lose your V plates.'

His smile widened. 'Worked, didn't it?'

'Yeah.' That was her, had been her, good for one thing only. Is that what he thought when he looked at her now? That she'd be an easy lay. The skinny teenager that she'd known had filled out into a man. He probably knew what he doing these days without her directing. It was tempting to find out.

She leaned on the hood and looked at him. 'Takes more than a beer these days, Gil.'

He rested his elbows on the hood too. 'What does it take?'

He'd all but admitted what he wanted. She looked away. It would be all too easy to fall into the back seat of his car again. The attraction hadn't faded. 'I'm not that girl.'

Yet coming here she realised that she was, on the inside. She still wanted to drag Gil into the dirt and have her way with him. She wanted to muck around and see how far he'd follow. Why couldn't she be sensible and do the right thing? Get her own halo, even if it was from the two-dollar shop.

'Let me get to know who you are now. You need a friend here.'

Her gaze snapped back to him. 'Or what, you'll tell people?'

'They won't hear it from me, Jasmine. I'm not that kind of guy. You know me.'

Did she? She hadn't seen him for ten years. They'd both grown up and changed. Most of her memories of him were good. Today had been good. Her life was good and a million miles away from what it would've been if she'd stayed. If she'd stayed, they'd have been over in weeks.

This time around she had days. Nothing could go wrong in a few days. She could have some fun. Love him and leave him. Finish what they'd started and say goodbye the way they should've. The idea was more appealing than it should be.

She opened the car door. 'Calvin will start thinking we've been taken by the River Man.'

'That would make your show exciting.'

Jasmine rolled her eyes. 'That's not the kind of excitement that I want.'

'What do you want?'

She glanced at him, but didn't need to answer that question. She'd seen that look in his eyes before. The ten years vanished and all she wanted was to feel his lips.

This was stupid.

All her hard work of putting distance between her and Bitterwood was unravelling. It was all Gil's fault. He'd gotten under her skin. Hell, maybe she'd never picked him out. He was a persistent splinter. Maybe it was just because of the way it had ended. They'd never had a chance to say goodbye.

She'd remember to say goodbye this time. And she'd mean it.

'Calvin will be waiting.' Jasmine got into the truck without waiting for Gil to reply.

He shook his head, then got in and they drove back to the house.

'So, seven at the bar across the road from the motel?' Gil asked as he parked out the front of the farmhouse.

She wanted to say yes, but there was her job to consider. 'Make it eight and I want info.' She smiled, but she meant it. Work was her shield. She was here for business, not pleasure.

No matter how good that pleasure looked in jeans.

'I'm here to help your show.'

Her smile tightened. This wasn't personal for him, no matter how flirty he got. He just wanted her to be onside to protect his precious town. Gil the golden boy who could do no wrong.

Would he really seduce her to make sure she said all the right words on camera?

The youth she'd known would have never done that—but perhaps she should see how far he'd be willing to go. The old shimmer of adrenaline raced over her skin at the idea of playing with Gil again.

# Chapter 4

The crew was eating in the diner up the road from the motel. She and Gil had eaten here once; well, they'd had fries and cola as that had been all they could afford between them, but it had been the closest thing to a date that any guy in Bitterwood had ever taken her on. She'd thought it romantic.

Now a romantic date usually involved a couple of hours of prep, lingerie and an expensive restaurant as her date tried to impress her—the first few times she had been impressed. Trouble was, she'd rather go to a sports bar and eat buffalo wings and beer than sip champagne and eat dainty.

She hadn't outrun all of her upbringing. She popped another fry in her mouth and listened to Luke talk about his day. Turned out there was no River Man lore before the first death, but now everyone knew about him and everyone knew to stay away from that part of the river.

'Well, the River Man didn't spontaneously evolve one night,' she said between fries. They were just as greasy as she remembered and she'd thrown on extra salt. Her burger was three-quarters eaten and was probably going to stay that way. There was only so much she could eat, unfortunately. She picked out the tomato and finished what she was calling a salad.

'This one is weird even for us.' Calvin shook his head. 'You eating the rest of that?'

Jasmine pushed the plate over. 'What did you learn?'

'That folks believe he's real. There's this edge of reverence and fear.' Calvin added between bites.

That was nothing new. Most people believed in their local monster no matter how unlikely it was. 'Gonna need more than that to fill an hour.'

Calvin took a drink to wash down the last of her burger. 'I'll get some interviews, the old-timers who remember and the youngsters who use the story to scare each other.'

'Scare?' That was new, but then when she'd been in high school the murder was still too real and fresh for anyone to be so careless. She shivered at the memory of the monster. It wasn't real. It couldn't be real. Yet when she closed her eyes, she saw him grabbing her uncle. The growling and the night closing in. She'd been so well hidden he hadn't seen her. She'd stayed still for so long her legs had cramped and insects had bitten her, but she'd been too afraid to swat them away in case movement drew their attention. Sweat formed and trickled down her back. That one memory still had the power to unsettle her stomach.

Think of the science. She forced out a breath.

She'd never seen a monster during the three seasons of this show.

Monsters weren't real ... but she knew what she'd seen.

'Oh yeah. Apparently the high school kids dare each other to swim across the river in the River Man's zone. How about you? You looked like you were interviewing our guide pretty thoroughly.'

'Just making nice with locals. Learning from the best.' She winked at Cal.

Luke shook his head. 'Guys, this has got to be a hoax. I know we told the committee it was probably cryptid—'

'How can it be a hoax when it goes back over a hundred years?' Calvin finished the last of her burger.

'Hoaxes have a purpose.' Even elaborate ones. Sometimes it was for notoriety of the witness, sometimes to scare, sometimes just for kicks. 'Besides, there are plenty of other amphibious men around the place. Or should I call them aquatic humans?' Whales had once been land dwellers, had humans gone back to the rivers?

Luke nodded. 'Yeah, but do any look like this one?'

'None of them match.' If they all looked the same, she'd have been naming a new species and writing up an article for a respected scientific journal, not working on a TV show that while it paid her bills, didn't exactly take her zoology career in the right direction. On the other hand, it did open other doors and she got to travel and have fun. 'I've got enough to do a sketch and talk possible biology.'

'I'm going to have to go with urban myth and look into how it started,' Luke said. 'Looks like covering the festival is going to be a good fluffy filler.'

'Myths don't kill on a semi-regular basis,' Jasmine said. This was like nothing they'd ever researched. It was too fresh and yet too old.

Neither of the men spoke. Neither looked happy.

'I know we have to do something with this ... but I don't know what. Cryptid might be the safest.'

'Act like it's real. Do you think it's real?' Luke watched her closely.

'I think something is killing.' That she was sure of. But it couldn't be a person because the time span was too long. Plus human serial killers didn't act like the River Man.

'That's bugged me too. No one seems that interested in investigating the deer mutilations.'

Jasmine tilted her head. 'We all knew the reason for that, don't we? Wouldn't be good for business.' The last thing she should be doing was trying to solve what the River Man was. But she wanted to know if only so she could put that childhood fear to bed. She finished her cola. 'On the subject of the committee, I have schmoozing to do.'

'Take one for the team.' Calvin raised his hand and Jasmine slapped it as she walked by.

She'd get the third-degree tomorrow—about what she'd learned, not about what had happened. Nothing was going to happen. Just a drink with Gil. 'Cause she'd always been able to keep her hands to herself around him. Maybe she didn't have to ... they were both adults.

\*\*\*

There'd been a moment when Gil had looked at Jasmine and time had stood still. It wasn't that he hadn't had any girlfriends since her, but being with Jasmine was exciting. She made his heart beat faster.

Once he would've claimed he'd dated her to piss off his father. The thrill of crossing the line and doing the wrong thing, but being with Jasmine hadn't felt wrong.

Now though ... he didn't know what it was.

He walked into the bar with a folder of photos and documents, not sure if he had gathered them for Jasmine, for himself, or the town.

She was waiting at a table, sipping a beer, alone. He'd half expected the other two guys to be with her. However, he was glad they weren't. She had a notebook on the table along with a tablet, and she was completely absorbed in what she was doing and oblivious to the curious glances of everyone else in the bar.

He was going to be interrupting her even though she was waiting for him. And everyone here would see them talking. He hesitated. What did it matter? No one knew who she was, all they would see was him talking to the TV show people.

With a determined stride, he crossed the floor and sat opposite her.

That made her glance up. It took a moment before she smiled; it was a professional smile though, not like the ones she'd given him this afternoon.

He put the file on the table. 'I don't know how helpful it will be, but I thought the old maps with owner details might help you form a better picture of what the town was like when the River Man first made an appearance. The history angle might give you something interesting?'

He'd really had no idea how much work went into an episode, but he was beginning to get the idea that they didn't roll into town and slap something together.

'That'll be great. There's no other lore so it will be nice to at least question and hypothesise how the River Man stories started. You won't get into trouble?'

'No, this is all requestable info and the mayor told me to help you.' He'd made sure that he wasn't going to get chewed out for handing over copies of the old town maps.

Her smile widened. 'Thank you. We were talking about this kind of stuff this afternoon.'

'You really do put effort into this.'

'Yeah.' She turned the paper toward him. 'At the moment I'm listing the locations and features of all river men-type creatures in North America. Amphibious humans could be a great special.' She showed him the tablet. 'This is me trying to group them by characteristics.'

He looked at the River Man's family tree. Bitterwood wasn't that special when compared to the rest of the country.

'What are the numbers?'

'The black is the number of sightings and the red is the number of human deaths attributed to the creature.'

Bitterwood had the highest kill rate by a long way. Not that that was anything to be proud of. 'And you've been doing this while you were waiting for me?'

'Not all of it.' She swiped to a different page. 'I keep a database of creatures. But I hadn't tried to group them as a genus or family before. It's kind of fun. I bet I could include other hominid branches, like sasquatch.'

'Like a deviant branch of human?'

'No, well, at least not for ones like the River Man, as they're amphibious.'

Gil raised his eyebrows. How did that separate them from human?

'We're mammals.' She pulled up a different screen. 'Different part of the tree to amphibians, but it could be convergent evolution—when different creatures evolve similar characteristics but aren't actually related.'

Gil nodded but wasn't entirely sure that he'd got a full handle on the idea, but then she did have a college degree in the subject. 'I'm going to take your word for it.'

'Probably a good idea because once I get started, I could go on forever. Not everyone's idea of small talk.' She closed down her tablet and stacked it with the folder of maps, but kept her notebook open.

A subtle reminder that this was supposed to be work.

Maybe he should've let her talk on about how to classify the creatures. There'd been a spark in her eye, the one that had once appeared when she was plotting trouble.

She'd changed and it felt as though he hadn't. Nothing here had.

'Did you want another beer?' He needed a drink. Maybe they had nothing to talk about. Had they ever had much to talk about?

'That would be great.'

He went over to the bar and ordered, knowing someone would say something.

'So you chatting up that TV host?' one of the old guys said as soon as the order had left Gil's lips.

'Talking about the River Man.'

'Sure you are.' He winked and looked in Jasmine's direction. 'Hoping to give her a private look at the river?'

He'd already done that ten years ago and he was a bit too old to park now. He was tempted to make a snappy comment, but whatever he said wouldn't matter as people had already made up their minds about what was happening. The arrival of the two beers saved him from making any comment.

'Well, we're apparently already sleeping together.' Gil said as he sat. Maybe he shouldn't have said anything to her, but she needed to know that nothing moved faster than gossip—still.

'If even half the rumours about me were true, I'd never have time to get any work done.'

He forced a smile. 'This is different, Jasmine. You know that.'

'They don't.' She picked up her drink. 'Don't worry, I won't damage your reputation, again.'

He looked at her for a moment. She had no idea what had happened after she'd left town. 'It never got damaged the first time. I moved out the next day. Moved in above the shop. I didn't speak to my father for months. Couldn't look at him.'

A frown formed on her face, as if she couldn't understand what he was saying.

'He went too far, but I didn't think that you'd actually leave.'

Jasmine leaned a little closer. 'I had no choice.' Her voice was low, but she glanced around as though well aware that people were looking for something to talk about. She probably recognised most of the people, even if she couldn't remember their names. 'Let's not do this here.'

'What?'

'They're going to talk anyway, so let's give them something to chew over.' Her lips curved, then she picked up her beer and finished it. 'Let's get out of here.' She lowered her voice, 'and find somewhere more private.'

There was no way that him seeing her was going to end up as anything but grist for the rumour mill, but he'd accepted that. However, leaving the bar with her? That would ramp up the scale of the gossip from bearable to all kinds of innuendo. It would take months for that to wear off, and even then he was sure it would be mentioned every time the River Man came up.

There would always be a conversation that began with, 'remember that TV show host...'

And if he said no and went home alone then all they would've been was business. Her smiles would cool and she wouldn't look at him like that again.

She lifted her eyebrows as she waited for his response.

He'd always been a sucker for her kind of trouble, but he wasn't ready to be seen taking her home. 'Want to walk down to the river?'

'To the scene of the crime?' She wasn't talking about the River Man now, she meant when his father had found them.

He nodded.

'Actually ... were victims attacked during the day or at night?' She put the file, her notebook and tablet into her backpack, then stood.

'I'm not sure. The bodies were found the next day.' They walked toward the door, and to anyone listening it was not a romantic conversation.

'Hmm, I might need to get the coroner's reports.'

'I don't see a problem with that.' Hopefully his father wouldn't either. 'I don't know what you'll find though.'

'There'll be an estimated time of death as well as a cause of death. It would be interesting to know. Most of the sightings have been at dusk. When have the deer been killed?'

'Harder to see in the gloom?' Now it sounded as though he wasn't quite a believer. He wasn't a scientist but there was too much evidence saying that something did exist. That there was a family tree for these types of things; he shivered as they stepped outside and it had nothing to do with the chill night air. 'Ranger thinks the deer were killed late afternoon.'

He knew the mutilations were becoming more frequent. He also knew that the mayor was doing his best to keep a lid on it. If they became too frequent, people would start to worry.

Jasmine put her backpack on, and they walked down the sidewalk.

'Did you want to stop at the motel? Put your bag down?'

'No, Cal and Luke will want to know everything, and I'm not ready for that yet.'

'I thought you didn't care about gossip.' He smiled when she shouldered him, a move that was familiar and had once been followed by more contact. Her hand in his or her arms around his neck and then her legs around his waist as he'd picked her up. The whole time she'd be asking if he was worried about what people were saying.

He'd pretended he hadn't worried what people were saying about them.

His friends had alternated between ribbing him for slumming it to asking what she was like in bed and if he'd hook them up when he was done. He'd levelled the guy who'd suggested that. No one had been so forward after that.

But they'd all been thinking it, wondering when he'd get bored so they could move in.

No one knew that he'd watched Jasmine for months before asking her out. It didn't matter what people said either to her face or behind her back, she'd just shrugged it off and done what she'd wanted. He'd envied that. She wasn't like everyone else. Like him.

However the comments from his friends had hurt him, and he'd felt bad for her.

'They're my colleagues. It's different. These people?' She waved her hand to indicate the town. 'Nah. If all they have to occupy themselves is to talk about what we're doing, they need to get a life.'

'Gossip is their life,' he said without a trace of humour.

'I know. How bad was it after...' she let the sentence hang as they passed a few other people.

Gil gave them a nod in greeting and let them move on before answering. 'It was uncomfortable. Your dad was convinced I'd done something to you. My dad was saying you'd probably just run away. There were a thousand different theories, a few involved the River Man taking you as a concubine. One of the pastors may have started that one to try and keep teenagers from parking by the river and getting busy.'

Jasmine laughed. 'Teenage girls you mean. But if all the teenage girls are keeping their panties on, who are all the teenage boys parking with?'

Gil opened his mouth then frowned. 'You know, I don't think anyone has asked that question before.'

'Maybe they should. Half the stories about me weren't true.' She shoved her hands into her pockets as they crossed the road and kept on walking. There was no sidewalk or streetlights now, just dirt and grass.

'And the other half?'

'They were more than enough to spark the stories.'

'I didn't gossip about you, us.'

'By the time I was with you, that ship had well and truly sailed. My reputation was doomed no matter what I did.'

'I wanted you to know that I didn't join in; however I should've told them what my dad had done when people asked where you were, but I was embarrassed and afraid of what he'd do if I did speak up.' Once the initial shock had worn off, he was ashamed that he'd said nothing. He stopped walking and faced her. The river was only twenty yards away, burbling in the background. 'I'm sorry I didn't stand up for you.'

'We were kids. I didn't expect you to. No one ever stood up for me.' She glanced away. 'I knew that what we were doing would end badly.'

'It didn't stop you though.'

'Or you.' Her eyes were dark as she looked at him. 'Why did you do it? Was it because you knew I was easy?'

He grimaced. He'd be lying if he denied that was part of it, but it wasn't all of it. And admitting that made him seem shallow ... and a dick. He had to say something and the longer he stayed silent the worse it would get.

'Gossip was like water off a duck's back to you. I wanted to know how you did that. That I'd heard a few stories certainly added the allure.'

His face was hot and he was glad it was dark so she wouldn't be able to see the extent of his discomfort.

'I have to admit there was a certain attraction to mucking around with the chief's son.' She smiled.

'And now?' He stepped closer. From the moment he'd learned that she was coming to Bitterwood, she'd been on his mind. He'd thought about her over the last ten years and had wondered what had happened. She'd been the one that had slipped away before he'd been ready to let her go. Before they'd ever really had a chance.

Maybe that was all they were ever going to get, but at least this time he'd know for sure. And this time he'd be ready to say goodbye when she left.

Jasmine would never be happy here. He couldn't imagine her helping to run his shop or sitting on the River Man Festival committee. He couldn't imagine anyone in town wanting her on any committee if they discovered who she was.

She lifted her hand and traced the lapel of his jacket. 'That attraction is still there.'

His heart kicked over. It wasn't him just hanging on to a brief but dramatic affair from ten years ago.

'But I'm only here for five days.' Her hand rested on his chest. 'Is it really a good idea to start something up?'

'Maybe we're just finishing what we started.'

She laughed. 'Yeah ... there was a lot left unfinished.'

He remembered too well the way her mouth had been on him, the scramble for a condom ... then the lights and the yelling. Someone must have snitched. It wasn't the first time they'd parked the car by the river. Where they were standing now had been a popular place for teens to come. Close enough to town that it didn't look bad, far enough that people wouldn't walk by. It was now a rest stop for travellers, complete with a picnic table, a rubbish bin and one lonely streetlight.

He took her hand and the finished their walk to the riverbank.

'Is the table named in our memory?'

'No, but it appeared less than six months later.' He knew that it hadn't had the desired effect. It had just given kids somewhere to hang out and drink the booze they'd pinched from their parents.

They sat at the picnic table and looked over the inky water. Frogs sang. They were barely out of town and yet it was quiet. He closed his eyes and breathed in. Her hand was warm in his.

'It hasn't changed that much, has it?' Her voice was soft.

'No. Not really. You have.' He hadn't.

'I'm kind of glad about what happened now. I know that sounds weird.'

He opened his eyes and looked at her. 'I get it. If you hadn't been pushed, you may not have learned how to fly.'

She nodded. 'We'd have broken up anyway and I'd have married some deadbeat like my dad and popped out a few babies. You'd have got engaged to some well-thought of girl who didn't misbehave as a hobby and she'd have given me the evils every time we passed in the shops.'

He knew she was probably right. By interfering, his father had given Gil a reason to rebel and not accept the way things had been ordained.

'But none of that stuff ever happened, Jasmine. And I'm glad. I don't think either of us would've been happy.'

'Would we have known what we were missing?' She moved so she was facing him, one leg on either side of the bench.

He turned as well; their knees were touching. He brushed her fingers and she grasped his hand again. 'I would've because I'd tasted freedom. You showed me what it could be like if I didn't listen to all the people telling me what I should be doing.'

And he was going to ignore all the warnings that said this was a really bad idea. He leaned in and kissed her. Maybe it was goodbye despite the lingering attraction. Maybe he was chasing old ghosts...

Then she kissed him back. It was just a small move but enough for him to know that she was thinking about more.

'What are we doing, Gil?' Her hand rested on his thigh and she hadn't pulled back.

'Finishing what we started.'

'It's going to end the same way, with me leaving town.'

'I know.' He didn't expect her to stay. He only knew that he couldn't pretend there was nothing between them. Once again she was in his life and shaking it up, and he was enjoying it even though he knew the ripples would leave nothing untouched.

He was a masochist. He had to be.

'But you're the one who has to live here. Wasn't it bad enough the first time for you?'

'I wouldn't be here if I didn't think you were worth the trouble.' This time there would be no trouble. They were both adults ... plus no one knew who she was.

'I knew there was a bad boy in there just waiting to get free.' She edged closer, draping her legs over his.

His hands slid around her waist. 'You think I've got them fooled?'

'Oh yeah,' she said between kisses.

\*\*\*

With his lips on hers, the last decade melted away. There had been no one quite like him in her life before or after. While she knew it wasn't a smart move to be kissing him again, she couldn't find a way to say no and walk away.

He pulled her closer and she crossed her legs behind him to keep her balance. His hands were under her jacket. She wanted to be peeling off his clothes to see how much had changed over the years. She wanted be feeling his skin beneath her hands.

She wanted him.

And that wasn't going to happen out here or like this.

'This is super awkward.' She wasn't a teen who was happy to grope anywhere. However there weren't many places they could go.

'It is a bit.' He conceded, but he didn't seem to mind. His hands kept moving and his lips found hers again. His tongue dipped into her mouth and tangled with hers.

If they were both naked, the position would be perfect...

She rolled her hips against him. 'We don't have to stay here.'

'Are you in a rush?'

*Yes.* 'Are you stalling?' Was this a set-up? She hated that she'd thought that. But she'd been there before. Never with Gil though. He'd never been one of those guys.

'I wanted to get to know you before I invited you back to my place.'

Apparently she really hadn't changed that much, as once again she was sitting on his lap. She slid her hand down his chest and then lower. 'That's a long walk through town.'

And it would get people talking. A drink in the bar was one thing and could be chalked up to work, but going to his place ... that was something different. She wasn't sure she was ready to do that, no matter how much her body thought it was a good idea. Gil was silent, as though thinking it through.

Then she realised from his words he hadn't planned on taking her back to his place tonight. If at all. 'You don't want to be seen with me.'

She drew her hand back. They were sitting out here well away from where anyone could see them or overhear.

He winced. 'I was with you at the bar.'

'That's different. You don't want to be seen taking me home.'

He glanced away for a split second. It was enough. She still was the girl that he couldn't take home, even though he lived alone—or at least he said he had.

Shit, she should've done some more digging. Any digging. And found out what he'd been up to for the last ten years. It was her job to research, and she'd let herself be swept off her feet again without bothering to look where she'd land.

'It's not that.' But there was a warning in his voice.

Jasmine untangled herself from his embrace. 'Really? What is it?'

He reached for her hand, but she snatched it back. She was not going to get sucked in.

'I meant what I said. I want to get to know you this time. All I got were glimpses last time because we were too young and too busy getting our clothes off. This time you want to do the same. Is that all you think I'm good for? A quick screw while you're on assignment? Is that how it works?'

'Is that what you think I do? You think I'm sleeping my way across the states? Checking each one off on a map?' Of course he did. It's what she'd always done before.

'I don't care what you do out there, but right now you're here. We're here. And we're treading the same old ground.'

'You wanted to do this. It wasn't just me.' He'd kissed her first. Hadn't he? He'd brought her here, which was a big ol' hint about what was on his mind. 'So what if we have a few days of fun?' She crossed her arms. 'It doesn't matter how well we get to know each other. Our lives are too different. I'll be gone in a few days.' And they were wasting time.

He looked up at her. He was still sitting on the bench. 'You know, in those first few weeks after you left, I used to wonder what would've happened if you'd gotten pregnant. We'd have married and been together.'

Jasmine didn't move. Did he really think that is what would've happened? Had he really missed her that much? She'd missed him and she had picked up the phone several times to call, but she'd been too damn scared of getting his father on the line. Given that Gil had moved out, she wouldn't have got to talk to him anyway. Not that it mattered because she'd never quite worked out what to say.

He wouldn't have followed her the way she'd dreamed because his life was here.

And she couldn't come back and put her family in danger with the chief.

Why was she doing this to herself? She would've been better off avoiding him.

'We both know that marriage was never on the cards. No matter what happened.' She could imagine the chief's face turning red. If catching them in the car had been bad, announcing an accidental pregnancy might have given him a stroke. 'We were kids.'

'We aren't anymore.'

'Yet here we are.' She swept her hand out, pointing to the river. What had she expected? That he'd wine her and dine her? Whisk her off her feet with dinner and dancing? She didn't even want that stuff. She wanted it to be easy.

Nothing between them was ever simple.

That hadn't changed.

But it had never stopped them before. Maybe realising that was part of being an adult. That sucked. Being a grown-up seemed to be mostly about paying bills and making sure that no fun was had.

He stood up but didn't touch her. She wanted him to touch her. When they were naked nothing else had ever mattered, but she didn't want Bitterwood looking at her like that again.

Somewhere along the way, she'd started to care about what people thought of her.

*Screw that.* She grabbed Gil's jacket and kissed him hard. 'Next time you invite me out, it had better end at your place.'

Before he could say anything, she started stomping back toward town.

# Chapter 5

After breakfast, Jasmine took the SUV and drove out to her mother's place. It wasn't something she'd planned on doing while here, but it was something that she should do. Her aunt was expecting her to visit and she couldn't face Tricia if she went back and said she hadn't stopped in. She owed Tricia this.

With the two guys busy setting themselves up for interviewing locals, she had taken the opportunity to go out. She'd told them that she'd be back within a couple of hours as she wanted to be there for the eyewitness accounts.

It was always fun to sort the attention seekers from the drunk visions from the ones who might have seen something. Some of the tales were amusing. What they wanted was a few articulate locals who would add to the show—aside from the mayor who wanted his five minutes while the festival was going, which he'd get.

The dirt driveway up to her parents' place hadn't changed. Maybe it had a few extra potholes. Her chest ached and for a moment she was that girl again. She closed her eyes. The one who walked home in her too tight winter shoes, her toes squished at the ends, and who was waiting for summer so she didn't have to wear any. By the time she was ten her older brother had started working, so there was a bit more money. Sometimes, when it was fruit-picking season, her dad would work and there'd be a little more money to go around—until he spent it or drank it.

She opened her eyes and stared at the house. There were chickens in the front yard in a pen that had seen many repairs. The yellow coat of paint she'd given it when she was twelve was peeling and faded. It didn't look like anyone had bothered to paint it since.

Why was she here?

What would she get out of it?

Nothing. Absolutely nothing. But her aunt would have her hide if she didn't stop in. Because she spent so much time on the road, she was still renting a room in her aunt's place. This was her family. And no one could pick their family.

It wasn't that she hated her family; she just hated what it had meant. Her whole life she'd been that Thorpe girl. When it had become clear that she wasn't going to fit in at school, or anywhere in town, she'd made sure that everyone knew she didn't care.

She had cared though. Few kids at school had played with her. Those who did were as bad off as she was. She used to look at the other kids' new clothes and new pencils on the first day of school each year with envy.

Now she could have as many damn pencils as she wanted.

Jasmine got out of the car and walked up to the house, testing the wooden step before putting her weight on it. It had been rotting when she'd moved out, age hadn't improved its condition. Then she knocked and waited.

Two kids peeked through the window. This was definitely the right house, so why were there kids?

'Coming,' her mother called out.

Jasmine winced. She'd been so busy running that she'd never stopped to look back at who she'd left behind. She'd been afraid they'd drag her back if she returned. That they'd stop her from leaving Bitterwood the way crabs would stop each other from escaping a bucket. No one got out, and everyone got dragged down. She wasn't a crab and she wouldn't get dragged back into this mess.

The door opened. Her mother's hair was all grey and her face more lined. 'Jasmine?'

'Yeah, Mom, it's me.' Her throat closed as she tried not to cry.

'Oh my Lord.' Her mother hugged her as though she thought Jasmine was going to slip free and run away. 'I never thought I'd see you again.' She drew back. 'You never came for Christmas or your brother's wedding.'

How could she explain her reasons? She'd been sixteen when she'd left. A kid having to make adult decisions. If Aunt Tricia hadn't been there for her to run to, she had no idea what would've happened to her.

'You never even said goodbye.' Her mother held her at arm's length.

'I had to go.' There was no point in pointing fingers now. 'I got into trouble and it was better that I go.' She'd kept her family safe. That was her other reason for not coming back. She had no idea how the chief would've reacted if she'd rolled back into town six months later, ready for Christmas. Tricia had come back for Christmas, like she always did, and Jasmine had spent Christmas drinking Tricia's brandy and eating a frozen turkey dinner.

Her mother shook her head but hugged her again. 'You were always my naughty one. Always asking questions and getting into trouble, and look where it got you.'

Jasmine couldn't tell if that was a compliment or condemnation.

'All educated, with a degree. First one in the family.' Her mother smiled and sighed. 'Well, we can't stand here all day. Come in.'

The house was small and dingy and smelled of tobacco, the way it always had. The two kids watched her with wide eyes, behind them in the living room the TV was on and the cartoons were chattering.

'This is your niece and nephew. Charley and Jay. I babysit during the day.'

'You still work at the school?' By second grade everyone had known that her mother was the cleaner. That had done nothing for her social standing.

Her mother nodded. 'Your dad can't work at all now. Bad heart.'

Jasmine bit the inside of her lip. She'd had more than one argument with her father. Once she'd started picking up odd jobs he'd asked for a share, she'd told him to get off his ass. She'd slept at a boyfriend's house that night.

And then more frequently.

That had definitely killed any semblance of respectability she'd had. Nice girls didn't sleepover. Nice girls didn't have sex.

And who exactly did those people think their precious sons were sleeping with? Each other? That it was somehow okay for the boy but not the girl had pissed her off. It still did. There was no biological reason for the double standard, just a social one. Bitterwood wasn't exactly progressive.

'Are you moving back?' Her mother looked hopeful—and old. She was barely fifty and she looked older than Tricia. Tricia was staring down retirement.

'I'm here with the TV show, Mom. We're doing a story on the River Man.'

'Oh.' She looked away and her hands twisted in her apron. 'Why would you want to do a show on that? It's just a story.'

'The TV show is about cryptids and the myths around them. You can see some clips online if you want.' She wanted to be able to share what she did with her mother, and for her mother to be proud of her. But from the look on her mother's face that wasn't going to happen. Her eyebrows pinched together and she shook her head.

'It's a bad idea, Jasmine. Don't go poking around. When Tricia said you were on a TV show, I thought it was a nice wildlife documentary. Not a show about monsters.'

'It is a documentary.' Why was her mother so upset at her looking into the River Man? 'We're only here for a few days. Talk to a few people, film some of the festival, talk about the myth and the biology of the creature.'

'What, like he's a real creature?'

Jasmine shrugged. 'That's where we start with every show.' Then, as they reviewed the evidence and eliminated things, they made their final conclusion. While many people speculated online, they tried to bring science and history together.

Her mother relaxed a little. 'Did you want tea? Dad will be on the back porch, he'll be glad to see you.'

Jasmine doubted that. He'd probably ask for a hand-out.

'Does Jason pay you for the babysitting?' Jasmine was willing to bet her brother wasn't offering their mother anything. He'd always been selfish.

'No, he's still at the cannery. His wife is too. How they met. The wedding was real pretty. I'll get out the pictures and bring them with the tea.' Her mother shooed her out the back door.

Her dad sat on a chair, legs outstretched and a packet of cigarettes on the table. Always money for them, even if it was just potatoes and a bit of ham for dinner. The school lunches had been her guaranteed meal and no matter how bad it had looked, she'd eaten it.

From here she could look across the paddock to her uncle's land. In the distance was the house and his workshop. He was a mechanic and fixed just about anything. In summer they'd traipsed across the field and fished. If they were lucky, they'd have a feast of fish for dinner. Her uncle had always warned them to be careful and always be home by dusk in case the River Man was hunting.

'Dad.' She didn't know what to say to him. All they'd done was argue before she'd been forced out of town. The terror of hitching to Seattle with nothing but what she was wearing had faded. Now she was glad that she'd left. If she saw the chief, she was going to thank him. That would piss him off. She smiled at the thought.

Yeah, she was going to make the effort to see him and do that.

Her father grunted. 'Got a nerve showing up here.'

'My job brought me here.' *You should try working.* It certainly wasn't her choice to be here. 'Mom looks tired. She could do with some help.' *Since you're sitting here like a lump.*

'Doc says I can't work.' He pulled out a cigarette and lit it.

Jasmine's fingers curled, but she resisted the urge to rip it out of his mouth. 'You could help look after the grandkids.'

'That's woman's work.'

'You married well, didn't you? Made sure you got a wife who'd do everything for you so you could sit back.' If he'd made an effort, then the family wouldn't be scraping by. But he didn't care. He was too lazy to care. She gritted her teeth against all the old anger that wanted to surge forth. All the times she'd bitten her tongue and done as she was told to make it easier for her mother.

'Don't speak to me like that.' He made to get up. 'You always had food and clothes.'

'Because of Mom.' Her mother would've been better off leaving him, but her mother was loyal. Plus leaving her husband would've made the family look worse. She'd probably have lost her job too. Bitterwood was like that, it didn't like single mothers or women who didn't conform. It was no wonder Tricia left as soon as she could.

All the reasons she hated Bitterwood bubbled to the surface. The small-minded busybodies who dictated who was in and who was out. Who should be scorned and who should be praised. Missed church, well you can be damn sure that it had been noted and it would be commented on.

She looked at her father and she understood why she'd never moved in with a man, or even let a relationship get too serious. She didn't want to wake up one day and see her husband was really a leech who expected a maid. While she couldn't remember her grandfather very well, it was entirely possible that Tricia hadn't married for exactly the same reason.

Her mother came out with tea and some cookies and the photo album.

'Isn't it nice Jasmine came to visit? She's all grown up and successful.' Mom smiled at Dad.

Dad grunted. 'Thought you were dead.'

'I grew up here. I doubt there's much that could kill me.' She was far too hard and chewy, and most people would agree.

That almost made him smile. He tapped his cigarette on the ashtray. 'How about helping us out now you've made it big. I could use a car.'

And there it was. Some things never changed. He wouldn't be getting a cent out of her. 'I have college debts and an old car myself.'

He turned to look at her, his eyes cold and hard. 'You always thought you were too good for us. Always trying to befriend the kids from the other side.'

'Jasmine always made lots of friends.' Her mother smiled, but it looked strained. The two little kids had followed her out, taken a cookie and scampered off to play in the field.

'Lost 'em too.' Her father added.

*I wonder why...*

'I wanted to see more of the world than Bitterwood.' That hadn't been true at first. She'd wanted to belong here once. To have people look at her and smile and nod instead of pretending to see through her; realising that would never happen had hurt.

Without the family baggage, she'd discovered who she was in Seattle. She'd thrived and grown. She looked at her parents and then her brother's kids. She'd outgrown Bitterwood. Had she been outgrowing it even before she was forced to leave? Maybe ... maybe that was why she'd been poking all the wrong beehives.

And yet at sixteen she'd still wanted to fit in so badly. Had she wanted Gil because he could help her fit in? And now? Was she still trying to fit in?

She accepted the cup of tea from her mother. 'You should come down to Seattle over the school holidays. Have a holiday, Mom.'

'Oh, I couldn't. Who'd look after the kids?' She shook her head, not even letting the idea take hold.

'Dad could manage, or I'm sure Jason could get someone else to babysit for a few days.'

Dad gave Mom a glare and then she shook her head and folded her hands in her lap. 'I don't think so, Jasmine, my place is here.'

Jasmine sipped her tea so she wouldn't say something that would start a fight or get her into trouble. But the words burned and knotted her stomach. She'd known that coming here would achieve nothing and she'd been proven correct.

Tricia always came home in a bad mood after visiting her family and it was obvious why.

'Didn't you ever want more?' Jasmine looked at her parents.

'More than what?' her mother asked.

'Just more.' There was more than being ground into the dirt. More than living on the fringes of a small town where everyone knew your family back several generations. The Thorpe stain went way back. Her mother's family, the Royles, were no better. But she couldn't say it. For some people, escaping your past was like treason. She'd betrayed her family by leaving and even though her mother had embraced her, there was still a distance and distrust.

'I have a house, a husband and family.' Her mother smiled and the lines in her face deepened.

'My sister is making you like her. It's not natural for a woman to be alone.' Dad grunted and took a second cookie. There'd been one each.

'You have it, dear.' Mom offered it to Jasmine.

If she said no, that would be rude. So she took the cookie while her mother went without. How often did her father take her mother's share and she just let him?

'You should come home more often, Jasmine. You'll want to settle down and have kids.' Her mother sipped her tea and looked hopeful.

There was no way in hell Jasmine would be doing that here. The idea of being stuck in Bitterwood for the rest of her life was enough to make her skin crawl. She had to fight the urge to get up and run for the car.

'I like the city.' She liked being one of many and able to disappear. 'I can't see myself ever moving back.'

'Just like Tricia. I told you no good would come from letting her sit at our table for Christmas. Filled her head with wrong ideas.' He pointed at Jasmine.

'And what's wrong with that, Dad? Is this the life you imagined having? What you hoped for when you were sixteen? You could've left like Tricia. Followed your sister and joined the military.' But that would have involved effort and she couldn't imagine her father ever striving for anything.

'Some of us had to work to help put food on the table. She ditched us without a backward glance.' He stood up and glared at her. 'Don't be coming back here to rub our faces in your money. We did the best we could.' He stomped inside.

*Mom did the best she could while dragging your carcass along.*

Jasmine knew that Tricia sent gifts to her nieces and nephews. Never money, but useful things like pencils and shoes and clothes. Her father hated that his sister never gave a hand-out to her siblings. There was no need for Tricia to be giving anything to anyone, but she didn't want more kids growing up the way she had. Would little Charley and Jay get out of Bitterwood, or would they be stuck here too? She watched them playing in the field. At the moment they didn't know any different. When they started school they would.

'Don't be so hard on him,' her mother murmured.

'Mom, he let you work while he did nothing.' All her childhood, that was what she remembered. Her mother cooking, cleaning, going to work and repeating every day. Dad would take money for cigarettes and beer. How many colouring pencils could she have had if he'd skipped one of his *necessities*?

'It wasn't always like that. After the lay-off, he lost part of himself.'

Jasmine reached into her handbag and pulled out all of the cash she'd taken out that morning. A hundred dollars. It wasn't much. 'I want you to buy yourself something, Mom. Not him, not the house, not the kids. You. When was the last time you treated yourself to anything?'

'I don't need anything.'

'Go out then, go to the movies with your friends. Treat them too.' She looked at her mother, knowing that what she was saying might as well be in another language. Her mother would spend the money on something other than herself.

Maybe Jasmine should buy her a movie ticket or send her a book or a new hat and coat for winter. Do what Tricia did to make sure the present was used by the recipient. Cash would get used by her father.

Her mother shook her head. 'I knew you weren't going to stick around. Even when you were little. It was like you couldn't wait to crawl, then walk and run. You wanted to jump into everything and try everything. You were never happy sitting. Some of us are happy to sit and watch the birds fly overhead ... we don't need to be one. But even birds visit once a year, Jasmine.'

That was as close to telling her off as her mother ever got.

Would it really be that hard to come here for Christmas? Five days, a week tops. All those Christmas movies about clashing families scrolled through her mind. Oh yeah. It would be just like that only it wouldn't be funny because it would be happening to her.

'I'd really appreciate it. Your dad would too. He had all the cops looking for you.' That must have put the chief in a tight spot. 'It was a relief when Tricia rang to say you were there. She was going to send you back.'

'What?' Her aunt had never mentioned that. She was so glad Tricia hadn't.

Her mother nodded. 'Dad wanted her to, but I knew you'd just leave again and it was better that you were with an adult we knew and trusted than you being on your own. Didn't stop us from worrying though.'

'I'm sorry, Mom.' She'd thought her parents would be glad to see her gone. One less mouth to feed. One less kid to tell off.

'You should've called.'

'I didn't want to be told to come home.' For the first two years that was exactly what she'd been afraid of. That was why she hadn't come back for Christmas. What if her parents had made her stay? Then she had gotten too busy to even think about coming back.

Her mother sighed. 'It's all old news now.'

And yet Jasmine knew that it wasn't forgotten or forgiven. Come Christmas time it would be fair game. Families. Life would be easier if you could pick them.

\*\*\*

Gil restocked the shelves and made notes about what he needed to reorder. There were several orders that he needed to box up ready for collection tomorrow as well. The door chimed and he glanced over.

His childhood friends Tyler and Angie walked over hand in hand. They'd been together for a couple of years and Gil knew it wouldn't be long before Tyler put a ring on her finger. Gil wouldn't wish that on anyone, but Tyler was too far gone to be saved. Angie had briefly dated Gil. After he'd dated Jasmine and she'd left, Angie had thought she could save his reputation and get her nails into him. It hadn't lasted more than a few months.

She'd been more interested in teasing him and playing games.

After Jasmine, the games had seemed petty. He wanted someone he could talk to and be honest with. Not someone who expected him to say only the right things and be seen with the right people.

Gil wiped his hands on his jeans. 'What's up? Looking to redecorate your place?'

Tyler had recently bought a house, a good family house on the right side of town. It couldn't be long now until the big announcement. Tyler was exactly what Angie had wanted but didn't find in Gil.

'Thought I'd stop in. See if you're going to get a night off anytime soon so I can get the guys around for a game.' Tyler smiled.

That was not why he was here. They both knew that, but no one jumped straight to the point. Except Jasmine. She'd call a spade a spade, and would then use it as a weapon and bury the body if needed. He grinned at the thought.

Maybe he did like women more dangerous than was safe.

Gil nodded. 'I'm sure I can squeeze in a poker night, after the festival.'

Tyler nodded. 'Sweet.'

Angie gave him a less than subtle elbow to the ribs.

'Is there a problem, Angie?' Gil didn't have time for her games.

She glanced away as though the idea of saying something bothered her. 'Tyler.'

Tyler rocked on his heels and didn't meet's Gil's gaze. 'Saw you out last night.'

Ah ... he had wondered how long that news would take to come back to him. Fifteen hours. Not bad. He was sure that if people had seen him kissing Jasmine it would've been less that twelve, maybe even breaking into single figures.

'And?' He wasn't going to volunteer anything. Tyler was his friend, but these days Gil kept much stricter personal boundaries. People didn't need to know everything about his life, even though they thought they did.

His grandfather had been thought of as gruff. Truth was he liked his privacy, and after Gran had died he'd enjoyed not having to talk to anyone. He'd grudgingly allowed Gil to move in on the condition that they played chess every night and that there was no chitchat.

It had become clear why after a few days. His grandfather was going deaf. But Gil had learned the value of silence and that not everything needed to be spoke aloud. His grandfather's hand on his shoulder after a long day in the shop had been worth more than a casual thanks.

The only time Gil had ever heard him raise his voice was when his son, Gil's father, had demanded that Gil move back home. It had been an eye-opening experience to hear his father, the Chief of Police, getting a dressing down for behaving badly. And that had been the last time anyone had mentioned Gil going home.

The shop, while now his, was still full of his grandfather. His grandfather had said he was a damn fool for not going after Jasmine if he cared. He didn't know where she'd gone, and he hadn't known how much he cared. Not back then.

Not now either.

But he sure as hell wasn't about to say anything to Tyler and Angie; Angie would run her mouth off to all of her friends.

'You know how people talk.' Tyler shrugged as though it was just a part of life.

Angie found her tongue. 'If you ever want to get married, you can't go chasing every bit of out-of-town skirt. People might start to think you don't like the locals.'

He stared at her for a moment. Maybe he didn't like the locals because they were constantly speculating about why he wasn't getting married. Or they were offering to set him up or introduce him, as if he couldn't find anyone on his own.

'I don't believe she was wearing a skirt, or that it was any of your business what we were doing.' He levelled a glare at Angie.

'Buddy...' Tyler tried again.

'Nah,' Gil shook his head. 'She's here for the TV show and I'm on the committee, end of story. Go and find your gossip elsewhere.'

'I was just going to suggest that you be more discreet.' Tyler smirked as though he saw straight though Gil's defence. 'I'll send you a text about the game.' Then he tugged on Angie's hand and they started toward the door.

Angie turned at the last moment. 'Isn't the presenter's name Jasmine?' She lowered her eyebrows as though thinking. 'Wasn't that the name of the slut in high school? Didn't you get caught with her in your car one time?'

Gil's fingers curled and he learned that seeing red wasn't just an expression. But he could almost hear his grandfather warning him not to rise to the gossip's bait.

He breathed in, then out.

But he couldn't let it slide by. He had to say something. He had to defend Jasmine without revealing what she was hiding. 'I have a thing for women with pretty names.'

Angie blinked, and then smiled all sugar to hide the razors. 'It's not her name you're interested in, Gil. If you aren't careful, no one in Bitterwood will ever want to settle down with you as they will all know exactly where you've been.'

She tossed her hair and walked out of his shop, hand in hand with his best friend.

The idea that all eligible females in Bitterwood would leave him the hell alone was decidedly appealing.

Usually he loved living in a place where he knew just about everyone ... but occasionally he wondered what it would be like to live in a city where no one knew who he was. He understood why Jasmine had run and never looked back.

And why she'd never stay.

No one would care who she'd become but they'd never let her forget who she'd been.

# Chapter 6

There were people lined up and talking to Cal and Luke when Jasmine got back into town. At the moment it was information gathering. There would be interviews later. Some would be filmed at the location of the sighting and others would be done when the festival started the day after tomorrow.

She was hoping to get some more details on the River Man. Had they all seen what she had seen as a child? She knew that the memory of a scared six-year-old couldn't be relied upon. Maybe her imagination had made it worse. Or maybe she'd listened to other people's stories and absorbed their words.

That was a risk in such a small town. People would talk and their observations would all became similar. Memories weren't reliable and there were no photos of the River Man.

She was still hoping to see if the police had any pictures of footprints ... or anything else relating to the creature. If they did, there was a chance that they may not share even if Gil was doing the legwork. Technically it was evidence in an unsolved murder. Several unsolved murders.

That was the weird thing she kept circling back to.

There were too many deaths for the usual cryptid.

What she really wanted to do was study the old maps again. What was the town like a hundred years ago when the River Man had first appeared? She also needed to speak with the ranger. She made a note on her pad to do that. Even if there were no deer carcasses to look at, the ranger was hopefully a reliable source.

Instead of heading out again, which would've been odd as she usually listened to the stories and the descriptions, she sat with the guys and listened to people talk about their experience or their cousin's experience. It was no different to any other stage one interview, except that she knew most of the people—if not by name then on sight.

What was unsettling was when one man came in to talk about the death of his friend. They'd been out together hunting. It had happened so fast. The creature had come out of nowhere. He'd fired some shots into the air, but the River Man hadn't been startled. Then it had been over, and his friend was gone and so was the River Man.

The worst bit was he'd been a suspect. The cops had thought he'd killed his friend. He'd lost his job and his most of his friends ... it had been a dark time. He hated the festival.

Jasmine took a description from the man and also confirmed where he'd seen the creature. His friend's heart had been ripped out. She remembered hearing about the death as a kid. It had been around the same time she'd seen the River Man. She'd stayed away from the river and her uncle's property for months, even though her cousins had called her a baby for being scared.

Some of the older folk remembered a previous death. Most attributed that to drinking and swimming in the river at dusk though, not the River Man. No one remembered if his heart had been missing or not. That was interesting, and disturbing. Had the creature not taken hearts until recently?

A man about a decade older than Jasmine swaggered in. He took his cap off and sat in front of the three of them. A faded bruise coloured one cheek. He grinned at the guys, then looked at her.

Her heart stopped. Her cousin Theo. And he'd clearly recognised her.

'Well if it isn't little Jasmine. You're in town and you haven't bothered to stop in and say hello?'

She swallowed hard. Cal and Luke were looking at her. She could feel their gazes burning her skin.

'Cat got your tongue? Didn't you tell your fancy friends this is where you were born?' Theo rested his elbows on the table between them. 'Bet there's a whole lot you didn't tell them about what you used to get up to here.'

She glared at him. How had he known she was back? Had her mother said something? She'd known going to see her parents was a mistake—even if it was one she had to make. What did Theo have to gain by outing her? Or was it just petty vengeance because she'd gotten out? Was he hoping to drag her back down and destroy everything she'd work for?

Never. She wouldn't let that happen.

She would never be trapped here the way her mother was.

*Damn it, Mom.*

'Do you have a River Man story?' she said as though she didn't know what he was talking about, but she was sweating. Her shirt was sticking to her back and her underarms were clammy. All the distance she'd put between herself and Bitterwood vanished.

A few words and she'd lost every mile and everything she'd fought for over the last ten years. She wasn't that girl anymore. Changing her name hadn't changed the way people remembered her.

Not that she cared. She didn't care what they thought. That was a lie. She had wanted to fit in to the town, but her family, made up of people like Theo, had made sure that would never happen. The Royles and Thorpes weren't the best citizens. If she couldn't fit in, then she was going to stand out. And she had. For all the wrong reasons.

While she didn't care what her cousin thought of her, she'd cared what her co-workers thought. She'd worked so hard to prove that she was one of them. That she wasn't some backwater brat who got lucky.

Theo's grin widened, as if he knew the damage he was causing to her reputation. 'Nah. I just wanted to say hi to my baby cousin.' He stood and put his cap on. 'Been nice seeing you, Jasmine. I hope you do right by Bitterwood this time.'

He walked out of the small meeting room in the council building. Luke followed him out and shut the door, after telling the waiting people they were having a five-minute break. Then he leaned against the door. 'What was that all about?'

Jasmine's mouth was dry. She couldn't lie her way out of this. Theo had made it quite clear that she'd been raised in Bitterwood and had family here.

Both of her colleagues were looking at her, waiting for an answer.

The riverbank was crumbling beneath her feet. She was going to sink and drown.

'That was my cousin.' Well, clearly Theo was. He'd said that. She swallowed and tried again. 'I was born here, but I moved away a decade ago.'

'Why didn't you say? We didn't need a tour. You know all this stuff.' Cal crossed his arms.

Jasmine shook her head. 'I left for a reason. My family isn't well respected or liked.' She looked away. 'I put all of this behind me and changed my name. When I saw that we were coming here, I started praying that no one would recognise me. I was hoping that they'd think I was dead and long gone.'

'You should've told us,' Luke said.

'Why? Do you share your past with us?' She turned to Cal. 'You'd just have wanted to get me in front of the camera. Look at that, the zoologist on the show grew up with a cryptid.'

'And do you have a River Man story, Jasmine ... if that is your name.' Cal was still watching her as if he expected her to suddenly morph into someone else.

'Jasmine is my name. I changed my surname, that's all.' Did she tell them about what she'd seen? If she didn't and something came out later, it would be worse. 'Yeah ... I saw him when I was six.'

Luke grinned. 'Get out. You saw a cryptid, then became a zoologist to study them?'

'It wasn't like that. And this is why I said nothing.'

'Then what was it like?' Cal hadn't uncrossed his arms. 'How much of what we know about you is a lie?'

'What you know is true. I do live in Seattle with my aunt. I was raised by her, but only after I turned sixteen. I became a zoologist because I like animals. They fascinate me. People are weird. As for being on the show, I applied because it paid more than the other jobs I'd been doing. I have student loans because I have no rich family to help me out. Shit, I'm the first person to even go to college from my extended family, and I can count on one hand the number who finished high school.' She shook her head. Once again she was having to justify her existence. Why couldn't people just accept her?

Luke looked at the ground. He was doing this because it was his passion—his family had enough money that it didn't matter what he did or how much he earned. His salary was probably pocket money.

'I'm sure my cousin will be blabbing all over town, so we either get on with our jobs or we make me the issue. I'd prefer the former.' Then she leaned back and waited. Her heart was hammering her ribs and her back was sweaty with fear. But the worst had happened. Bitterwood would know who she was now, so there was nothing left to fear.

She pressed her lips together to stop the smile from forming. Let them see how far she'd come since leaving the small town and their narrow minds. She wasn't embarrassed about who she'd become.

'It's a shock, Jasmine.' Luke finally spoke. 'But I can see why you'd want to move on.'

'You still should have said something. Damn, Jasmine. It would've made things quicker if we'd known.' Cal shook his head.

'No it wouldn't, because as far as I know the mayor doesn't know who I am.' And when he found out things might get difficult.

'Is that going to be a problem?' Cal turned to face her.

'No, but when the Chief of Police realises...' she grimaced.

Luke frowned. 'Why exactly did you leave?'

She really didn't want to go into details. 'You know our guide?'

Cal groaned. 'I knew you were looking too friendly with him.'

'We had a thing in high school that didn't end so well. He's the chief's son.'

'And he knew who you were straight away.' Luke shook his head. 'What made you think he wouldn't reveal the truth?'

Jasmine gave a bitter laugh. 'Do I really need to answer that?'

'No. I think we've got it. And if I don't, I don't want the details about you and him. The question is, what do we do now?' Cal uncrossed his arms and leaned on the table.

'I vote for getting on with it. If someone makes it an issue, we deal with it then.' Luke shrugged. 'Yeah?'

'That's about the only option we have.' Cal didn't sound enthused.

'And if I'd told you before, that would still be the only option. This is about the River Man, not me.' She hoped her troublemaking cousin fell in the river and accidentally got taken by the creature.

*\*\*\**

As Gil was sweeping the floor—the last thing he did at the end of every day before locking the shop door—his father walked in. The festival was always a busy time for the police because of the influx of visitors. However it was unlikely Dad needed anything from the shop, and if he did he usually sent Mom.

'How's it going?' His father cast a quick glance around, as if noting the lack of customers. It was the end of the day and most people didn't stop in at closing time. The last-minute shoppers had left ten minutes ago and most of them had been picking up orders they'd placed by phone.

Tonight he'd print any online orders and box them up tomorrow ready for collection. He liked his routine. Everything worked.

'Good. You here for hardware?' Gil leaned on the broom. His dad was all grey now, and getting heavier every time he saw him. Gil had been his dad's height at sixteen, now he was six inches taller and a hell of a lot fitter.

Why had his father seemed so scary as teen?

Maybe all kids were afraid of their parents and getting into trouble. Except Jasmine.

'No, just wanted to stop in and see how it's going with that TV show crew.'

'Fine. They're interested in the stories, but that's their job. They make everyone interested and question if these things really exist or not.'

'That right? You seem to know a lot about them.' His father fixed him with a stare that had worked ten years ago but not since.

'I've seen a few episodes and I'm their committee liaison.' Gil finished pushing the dust around then swept it up. He knew where this was leading. Angie had the biggest mouth in town and had run straight to his father. Had it been her who'd made sure Jasmine and he were caught ten years ago? He didn't want to believe it, but someone must have said something.

His father followed Gil to the trash can. 'You've been seen with the woman.'

Gil emptied the pan and turned around, determined to keep his cool and not let his father get under his skin. 'And? What does it matter what I do?'

'People talk,' his father nodded, like that was all the answer Gil should need or want.

'Then maybe they should mind their own damn business.' His life was not that exciting. Obviously neither was anyone else's if all they had to talk about what he was up to.

His father watched him for a moment. 'Wherever that girl goes she brings trouble. Her whole family is trouble. I thought you'd learned that lesson.'

Cold traced over Gil's skin. Jasmine's secret was out. If his father knew, then everyone would know. He cursed Angie, and then Tyler for being such a goddamn sucker for falling for her.

'I don't think it's any of your business who I see. I thought you'd understand that by now.' He kept his voice cool and level. He would not give his father the satisfaction of seeing how much it bothered him.

'I'm doing you a favour, son.'

'How so? I knew it was her from the moment I researched the TV show. I looked forward to seeing her again. After what you did, you should be glad that she survived.'

'What I did? I made sure that she didn't drag you into the mud. People like that only ever drag others down.'

'Can you hear yourself? She is the host of a TV show. She is successful despite what everyone thought of her.' Once she'd left Bitterwood, she'd no longer been trapped by old bias; how deeply it truly ran.

'And you think that changes who she is? She used you last time and she'll do it again. Mark my words.' Dad put his hands on his hips as if what he said was indisputable.

Gil swallowed and tried to push down the anger that was spreading like acid through his veins. 'You had no right to interfere ten years ago and you have less right to interfere now. I'll do what I damn well please with whoever I damn well please.'

His father stepped back. 'The town is talking. She tricked them into welcoming her back.'

'No she didn't. She came for work. What the gossips don't like is that she didn't come back wearing a scarlet letter and with her cap in her hand begging forgiveness. This time her crime is being successful, and it just eats some folk up.' Gil crossed his arms. 'I say good on her.'

He stared at his father, daring him to say something else.

His dad grunted. 'People won't forget a second time. You'll ruin yourself and what you love.' His father swept his hand out to indicate the shop.

Was that a veiled threat? 'And you'll make sure of that, will you? You ran her out of town, will you do the same to me?'

His father's eyes widened for a moment. 'You're too damn stubborn. The more you shouldn't have something, the more you want it. Don't come crying when she ruins your life.'

With that final parting shot, his father yanked open the door with a jangle and then slammed it closed. Gil walked over and locked it, then flicked the sign over even though people knew his opening hours.

The shop and the town were suddenly too small and were closing in around him. They would all be watching and waiting to see what happened next.

Well, he'd give them something to get all worked up about.

\*\*\*

Jasmine, Cal and Luke walked out of the council office after spending all afternoon listening to people tell their tales. For the most part it had gone smoothly. Most people had said nothing about who she was, but she knew the whispers would be happening. They walked back through town to the motel. Her phone buzzed.

*Want to get dinner?*

She should say no. Having dinner with Gil would only add fuel to the fire. On the other hand, what did she care? He might though.

*People know. My cousin outed me.*

*Not just him. Remember Angie Dean from school? She stopped by with suspicions.*

Angie ... was she the redhead who had always worn nail polish and acted as though she was waiting for a talent scout to come past and notice her? It was flattering that so many people remembered her—and obviously still cared about what she did.

Jasmine glanced at Cal and Luke. 'Do you guys mind if I head out? I'm going to spend tomorrow afternoon visiting the ranger and then out in the field with the camera crew doing my bit, but I'll be around in the morning if you need me.'

Cal glanced at her and shook his head. He couldn't say much as he often bailed on Luke and her because a better offer had come up in a short skirt.

Luke smiled. 'Someone has to keep the locals on side.'

She laughed. Yeah, if only it was that easy. But she texted Gil and he offered to come to the motel so they could walk to the little Italian place that had been a fish and chip shop when she'd lived here.

Red and blue lights flashed from the car park as they drew closer. There were cop cars at the motel. The three of them stopped and stared. Jasmine sighed. What were the odds that it was unrelated to them being in town?

'This doesn't look good.' Cal walked a little faster.

Their rental SUV now had slashed tyres and words sprayed up the side, 'The River Man will get you', all the windows had been smashed.

It wasn't the first threat they'd received. Or the first lot of property damage. Some towns really loved their creature and didn't want anyone investigating it. But the timing of this was bad, as though it was a stab at her.

Calvin looked at her. 'They really do love you, don't they?'

'It may have nothing to do with me and more to do with the poking around we've been doing. I don't think what's here is a cryptid.' The River Man didn't fit the pattern.

Luke gave a slow nod. 'There's no ancient lore.'

'If it's a hoax, it's been running for a hundred years and that makes no sense.' Calvin shoved his hands into his pockets as the cop in charge walked over.

Jasmine's heart sank at the sight of Chief Easton. 'If it's a hoax, we already know that the person, or persons, behind it is willing to kill.'

'If it's a hoax, why haven't the cops caught the killer?' Luke was frowning. 'I know myths have power ... but...' he let the idea go as Chief Easton drew closer and introduced himself.

'Jasmine Thorpe.' The chief smirked.

'It's Heydon now.' She smiled sweetly. She wasn't going to lose her cool in front of him.

The chief immediately turned his attention to her colleagues and tried to extract facts and gossip. Both Luke and Calvin knew how to handle themselves.

She wanted to know if anything had been taken out of the car—or their rooms. From where she was standing she could see the room doors were closed, but that didn't mean anything.

'With all due respect, Chief, we aren't the ones under investigation.' Luke cut across what Chief Easton had been saying.

Jasmine winced on the inside.

'Of course you aren't. And I will do everything I can to catch the vandal, but with so many people—teenagers,' he slid a sly glance at Jasmine, 'in town it will be hard. Some people have no respect for the law.'

Jasmine's fingers curled. That had been for her benefit. Did he think that she'd slept her way onto the TV show? She'd been to college and had a degree. None of that mattered at that moment though, as she felt like the teen with trouble stamped across the ass of her track pants.

'Geez ... what's going on here?'

Jasmine turned at the sound of Gil's voice and shrugged. 'Nothing that hasn't happened before. Didn't this happen in Jersey?'

Luke nodded. 'Yep. A couple of college kids who thought they were defending the honour of the Jersey Devil.'

'So you make friends wherever you go?' Chief made another note in his book, but Jasmine had seen the look he gave his son.

Gil put his hand on the small of her back.

He wasn't going to back away this time. Not that he had the first time. There had been yelling, and a scramble for clothing. But he hadn't exactly stood up for her either while his father had called her names. She took a step forward, breaking the contact.

She didn't need him.

No, but she wanted him the same as always. One glance and lust made her blood heat. One touch and her skin was aching. One kiss and she was hoping for more.

Is that what he was thinking?

He'd made it pretty clear that he was interested in her when they were alone, that he wanted her. That he wanted to get to know her when they only had days was frustrating. She glanced over her shoulder; they were supposed to be going for dinner. That would be public. And he didn't care that people knew who she was. He was here even though the locals were gathering for some excitement. Would he still be keen to be seen walking to dinner with her? No doubt he'd expected a much quieter evening.

So had she. She'd been hoping for one that ended up with a lot less clothing.

'Is there anything else you need from us?' Jasmine put one hand on her hip and waited for the chief to look at her.

He didn't make eye contact; he instead spoke to Luke. 'If I could get a list of things that were taken, if anything. I'll give you a report number to give to the rental car company.'

'This will slow us down.' Luke's features were drawn into a frown.

'The committee will help in any way we can. I hope you won't judge the town by a few troublemakers.' Gil was next to her again, too close for it to be called casual. 'Most people are really interested in what you'll uncover about the River Man.'

Jasmine wasn't so sure about that anymore. They'd told the committee that it was probably a cryptid, but it was looking more like a hoax. What would Gil think of that? A hoax meant that someone in town knew what was going on and someone in town was a killer. And it had been going on for a century.

She shivered.

Her memory of the River Man replayed. Her uncle had fought off a killer. Why had he never said anything? Maybe he had and she'd been too young to know, or maybe he just didn't want the cops poking around. Her uncle hated authority of all kinds.

As much as she didn't like him, they had that in common. Maybe she should go and see him. He hadn't come in to talk about the River Man and he'd seen it. He must have a story to tell.

There were about twenty people gathered now. She could imagine the gossip was already flowing. This would be like throwing fat on the fire.

This was deliberate and connected. She cursed Theo for making trouble, but couldn't open her mouth to dob him in. Family loyalty. No, it was lack of proof and she had no faith in the chief. She hadn't forgotten his threat to her family, and she wasn't going to make it easy for him to follow through on his threat by pointing the finger at Theo.

Would the chief follow through though?

Surely not. It had been ten years.

But ten years meant nothing here. Old hatreds didn't die, they were handed down with each generation.

The chief kept them standing there for a few more minutes. Talking about the show, wanting to know who they'd spoken to and if they'd received any threats or had any enemies. The chief had managed to look at her for that one.

Luke slapped on a grin. 'I think we got this, Jasmine, why don't you head on off to dinner. Wouldn't want you to miss your booking.' He gave her a wink.

In that moment she knew he understood exactly why she'd kept her life in Bitterwood a secret. Luke had decided that he didn't like the chief any more than she did. However Luke knew how to play with authority. People who had money for lawyers obviously felt more confident than normal people.

Calvin would just yes sir, no sir his way through any difficulty. He tried to avoid confrontation. He'd be hating this. He'd be blaming her.

And he'd be right.

Jasmine didn't wait for anyone to disagree. 'Thanks, Luke. I'll see you in the morning.'

She had no plans to come back early tonight.

Before the chief could argue, she turned to Gil. 'Shall we?' Then she lowered her voice. 'Or is it getting too hot for you?'

He glanced at the crowd. 'It's a little warmer than I'd expected.'

'Well, let's just walk out of the car park while you make committee noises and we can pretend it's all official.' There was a slight bite to her words.

He shook his head. 'Nah ... because they'll see us go into the restaurant and no one would believe it anyway, not with all the gossip flying around.' He reached for her hand and she let him hold it.

For a moment they were teens again, knowing the town would talk but not caring.

They were older ... they should be wiser.

# Chapter 7

Gil tried to ignore the looks as they went past. If they didn't know who Jasmine was now, they would soon. Then what? They'd assume he was picking up where he left off ... or that he was indulging in a quick fling.

Both of which were true. He didn't know where this was going and he didn't care. With Jasmine there had never been any pressure to label what they had. Dating, going steady, exclusive? His last girlfriend had thought that dating for two years meant they were going to get engaged. He'd heard from a friend that she'd been saying it was only a matter of time until he popped the question.

He'd surprised her with a break-up instead. He hadn't been thinking marriage. He'd thought they'd been having a good time and that was all. And no one was forcing him down the aisle. He didn't care how appropriate it was, or timely.

The crowd parted; he tried to ignore the way people turned to watch. Once they turned the corner, they were almost alone. He let out a sigh. 'That was more of an audience than I was expecting.'

'You know me, it's all about how much attention I can get.' She grinned.

She was joking, at least he hoped she was. 'I'm pretty sure you didn't slash the tires just for me.'

'No, but after the day I've had, I should've been expecting it.'

'You think someone did it because of who you are?' He found that hard to believe. People hadn't hated her even though they hadn't liked her, but that was only because of her family. And the way she had refused to fit in.

He'd always liked that about her. While he was doing as he was told, she was free. She'd been the only freedom he'd had. When she'd left, he'd refused to go back to the way things had been. He couldn't go back, not after he'd tasted freedom.

She shrugged. 'Could be a co-incidence. Pretty sure your dad thought it was related.'

He'd noticed that too. His father had made no secret of not liking the fact

Jasmine was back, and worse, pursuing him again. Although it was more him doing the pursuing this time.

'Dad will do his job. I'm sure he'll find out who it was.'

Jasmine snorted. 'As he said, there's a lot of folk in town.' But she didn't sound as though she believed that. They walked a little further in silence. 'How about you? You said you had a visit.'

Gil nodded. 'Yeah. Tyler and Angie stopped by to remind me that people will talk and that I will be un-dateable if I carry on seeing you.'

'You sound really worried.' She tried to be serious and failed.

He wasn't worried. It wasn't that he didn't want to get married. It just wasn't high on his list. Plus he didn't like the pressure he was starting to feel from his mother, and his friends who were starting to settle down.

He gave a shrug. 'What about you?'

'What about me? I'm too busy to date. Never in the same spot for long enough.'

'A different guy in every city.'

She laughed. Not the giggle of a woman who was conscious about who was watching, but the full laugh of a woman who didn't give a damn if people thought she was loud.

'God, I wish.' She bumped his arm. 'You offering to be my good time while I'm here?'

Yeah. He was. Why the hell not. He wanted a good time. 'We always used to have a good time.'

She went quiet as she looked at him. 'Gil, you don't get to leave at the end. I do.'

'I know and I'm okay with that.' She'd outgrown the town, but he hadn't outgrown her.

'Geez, now that we've established where tonight is going to end up, what are we going to talk about over dinner?' But she was grinning, her step bouncier as she moved closer.

'Bitterwood history?'

She should be doing exactly that. 'I am tired of talking about the River Man.'

He glanced at her. 'I was thinking horse rustling.'

'Horse rustling?'

Gil nodded. 'Was quite a big business back in the day, apparently.'

'And how did you find that out?'

'Old Mrs Rogers came in to pick up her order of wire and for a chat over tea.' The older customers appreciated the way he listened, unlike other young folk. 'It was pretty easy to turn the conversation from her great-grandkids to what Bitterwood was like when she was a kid.' He opened the restaurant door for her. He'd spent the best part of an hour listening to the old woman talk. She had been more than happy to talk about her childhood, but she had no time for the River Man, said it was just people being reckless or drunk or both.

They were shown to their table, and for a few minutes conversation became more mundane. What do you recommend? Shall we get a bottle of wine or by the glass? Garlic bread? She'd insisted and he'd agreed. At least they'd both be garlicky.

He couldn't stop the smile from forming as they ordered. It felt right. It wasn't hard work or dancing around each other.

They knew each other, and even though they had done some growing up there was still enough there that she didn't feel like a stranger.

'What are you grinning about?' But she was also smiling.

'I never thought we'd be sitting here.' He'd never have imagined that her life would be so ... exciting. Her life was so far removed from this small town.

'Me either.'

'You must've known that the TV show would eventually come here.'

'Yeah, but I tried not to think about it.' She fiddled with her water glass. 'I'd hoped to get in and get out without being identified.'

'And Angie blew that for you.' If he hadn't wanted to see her, have a drink or dinner with her, people may not have started looking closer. Angie wouldn't have started getting nosy. Who was he fooling? Being nosy was Angie's hobby.

She looked at him for several seconds. 'I'd have been sad if you hadn't recognised me. It would've meant that I'd meant nothing to you.'

For a moment he saw a shimmer of doubt, but it was quickly hidden.

Had she really thought that she'd left no impression on him or his life? She'd woken him up and shaken him around. If not for her, he'd have happily plodded along until one day he arrived at a midlife crisis and realised he was miserable. At least he hoped he'd have eventually realised. The alternative was horrible. He might have wasted his life living it for someone else instead of himself.

The waiter arrived with the garlic bread before he could say anything. Not that he'd been sure what to say anyway. They weren't having a relationship. They were having an affair—a break from reality. Getting maudlin about the past wasn't going to help move things forward.

'So why do you think I'd be interested in horse rustling?' She picked up a piece of bread and took a bite. She obviously wasn't afraid of carbs.

'You wanted to know some history about the town.'

She raised an eyebrow. 'I don't want the whole history ... just the bits that relate to the River Man.'

'What makes you think it isn't connected?'

'I don't see how it could be.'

'Mrs Rogers seemed sure that it was. Don't steal horses or the River Man will get you kind of games were around when she was a kid.' He sipped his wine. He'd found that interesting. By the time he and Jasmine were kids there were no games. They'd been warned to stay away from the river. A fresh murder had put everyone on edge.

He remembered his dad talking about it. Of having no idea who the killer was, when even the only witness had been babbling about the River Man.

Jasmine finished her bread, a frown forming with each bite. 'Gil, there is a possibility this is a hoax of some kind.'

'Who keeps a hoax going for that long?'

'I don't know, but it's something we are considering. As a committee member I thought you should know.'

He wasn't sure that he was a believer in the River Man, but he knew the festival was good for the town. If it was revealed as a hoax, what then? 'Anything else I should know?'

She sipped her wine. 'I saw him.'

'What? Who?' Did she mean the River Man?

'I saw him when I was a kid around the time of the murder.'

He blinked and stared at her. 'You never said anything.'

'I was six and I was terrified. I'm not sure what I saw, but I'm glad it didn't see me.'

'How can you call it hoax?' She'd seen it. Was she here to put old nightmares to rest and prove that monsters aren't real? But if the River Man was a hoax then it was a person doing the killing. He'd seen the deer and the thought made him sick; better to believe in the monster than admit one lived in town.

'Because it shouldn't exist. I know the science. I have to trust the science.' Her voice was firm.

'And what does the science say?' He knew the answer already. If the River Man was real there would be more deaths on a regular basis and more sightings. There were fishers and hunters in the area, but no regular sightings.

'That it has to be a hoax. Myths don't kill, and there is no local lore that predates the first kill a century ago ... does that tie in with your horse rustlers?'

'It could be a cryptid.' But he didn't believe that either. What little belief he'd had unravelled. She was right. But no one in Bitterwood would want to listen.

'Then where are the others, the babies, the carcasses from them hunting and feeding?'

'He's vegetarian most of the time?' He shrugged. 'I know it makes no sense, but that is the fun of a cryptid.' If the TV show destroyed the River Man then the festival would die. It would be a stab through the heart of Bitterwood.

'Fun until it's your job to put it in a neat box with a label.' She took a bigger drink of wine and a waiter came by to top up her glass. When she'd gone, Jasmine leaned forward. 'If I screw this up, everyone will think I did it to get revenge on the town that booted me out.'

He was about to argue, but that was exactly what it would look like. Now her secret was out, there would be no graceful exit. 'You saw it.'

'Did I? I thought I did but maybe I was wrong.'

Their meals arrived. They'd both ordered pasta. She'd gone for something with chili and seafood, while he'd gone for his usual of lasagne with fries and salad.

'How weird is this?'

'What, us together?' He hadn't been finding it that weird. He'd been enjoying it.

'Yeah. Being back here is weird. It's like nothing has changed except me, but while I know that I've changed, no one else can see it. If I was naked it would be one of those nightmares.'

He stopped eating fork halfway to his mouth. 'Maybe you shouldn't come back to my place if you have a fear about being naked.'

He didn't want to be part of her nightmare. Did she really think he hadn't changed? Had he? He thought he had.

Then she grinned. 'Getting naked with you was never a nightmare, except that one time.'

'Let's not talk about that.'

Her leg brushed against his. 'We have unfinished business from that night.'

Gil drew in a breath. 'Yeah.' But he hoped he'd learned a few tricks since the last time he'd been with her. 'That's not why I suggested dinner though.'

'You didn't owe me dinner, or wine.'

He wasn't sure what she was saying. Would she have gone back to his place without dinner first?

'But I like it.' She spun her glass. 'You were the only person I really missed when I left.'

He doubted that. 'What about your family?'

'That's not the same. I have to like them. I should've hated you. But I never did.' Her lips curved in a wicked grin. 'Did you ever make peace with your father?'

Gil shook his head. 'No. He's never apologised. We talk, but it's strained. Have you seen your parents?' He couldn't imagine not seeing or speaking to his parents for ten years, yet he knew that's what Jasmine had done.

She'd cut off Bitterwood like it was a diseased tree branch.

'Yes.' She pushed a piece of pasta around before stabbing it. 'Do you think the legend started to cover up the trails of the horse rustlers? Will the old maps have the horse trails?'

He shrugged. 'Maybe. But why keep it going? That's the part that doesn't make sense if it's a hoax.' He didn't want it to be a hoax. Bitterwood needed its creature. Bitterwood didn't need a killer and deer mutilator.

\*\*\*

Gil lived above the shop now. She knew his grandfather had once lived here, and it looked as though he still did. The furniture was old, as though Gil hadn't been bothered to update the place to make it look as though he lived here.

'It's not much.' Gil put his keys on the hook by the door.

'It's cosy.' And not at all what she'd expected from Gil. She'd thought his place would be more modern somehow. The half a bottle of wine buzzed through her blood. Nerves wrapped around her stomach. She probably shouldn't be here, but she couldn't resist Gil, she'd never been able to.

He gave her a small smile. 'I know it looks like an old person's apartment.'

Her lips curved. 'No time to redecorate?'

'That and I didn't know what to do with it ... so I thought I'd leave it until I felt inspired. I'll give you the grand tour.'

The tour took about three minutes. There was one bathroom, two bedrooms, possibly a third up in the roof but it was being used for storage. The rest of the apartment was made up of living spaces. As they went around, Gil drew the curtains.

'Did you want a drink?' he asked when they made it back to the kitchen.

The tension between them was getting strained. They'd done this before, it shouldn't be this awkward. Maybe it was awkward because they'd done this before.

'No.' She took a step toward him.

Gil pulled her close. His lips brushed hers. 'I don't want to rush this.'

They didn't really have a choice. They had days, that was all. They both knew it could never be more.

'I've been waiting ten years.' She didn't realise how true that was until the words left her mouth. She'd been hoping to see him again—part out of longing for what they'd once had and part out of fear that he'd remember exactly what they'd had. But time had been kind to their memories.

He didn't say that she could've come back anytime. If she'd come back sooner, she wouldn't have been ready to face him. She wouldn't have been who she was now. It was only now she was able to keep her head high and glare down the gossips who'd wanted her to fail.

He deserved better than being the centre of the last round of gossip, but he'd chosen her. Again. He could've had anyone.

Her hand slid under his shirt. His skin was warm beneath her fingertips. He was familiar, yet strange. Not the boy she'd left behind, but there were glimpses of him. He'd been tempered by what his father had done and was stronger for it. Did he understand that his father had done them both a favour and made them better people?

His kisses deepened and they shrugged out of clothing, leaving shirts and jeans on the wooden floor. She almost tripped on the edge of a rug as they made it to his bedroom. His bed was huge, leaving only a foot of space around the edges. This piece of furniture wasn't old—so perhaps he was in the process of updating the apartment.

She sprawled in the middle. 'Why the ocean of sheets?'

'Because.' He crawled over her. 'I spent too many years sleeping in a single bed where my toes touched the end without me even stretching.' He kissed her again, then worked his way down her throat, to her collarbone. 'Now I can spread out.'

She did her best starfish impersonation and her fingers didn't reach the sides. She was about to make a joke about him overcompensating, but she knew that was a lie. Even at sixteen she'd seen enough naked guys to know he didn't need to worry in that department. 'I like it.'

She liked him. She'd wondered if the old chemistry would still be there or if it had been a fond memory, but it was still there. She shivered at his touch as his kisses went lower. Then he drew her panties down. Nice sensible cotton briefs, because that was what she travelled with. She rarely picked up when working. That wasn't what she did.

He didn't say a word about her underwear—smart man. He kissed the crease of her inner thigh and she held her breath.

'I think what we had was pretty one-sided back then.' His finger traced over her belly to her mound, then dipped lower.

She closed her eyes and swallowed. It had been. She'd given him his first head job, introduced him to sex. But they'd never gotten around to him going down on her. It had been another three years later before a guy had done that.

He pulled her panties all the way off and settled between her legs. 'I think I owe you one ... at least.'

'At least.' But then she couldn't put thoughts together. Her nails pressed into his shoulders. She was drowning in the roiling lust. And she let herself be swept away.

\*\*\*

Gil handed over the receipt to the camper who'd forgotten his tent pegs. The town was getting full and he was getting extra business, but he always did this time of year. He made sure to stock up on tent pegs and camp stoves and other camping paraphernalia in the lead up to the festival.

Nancy from the committee bustled her way in. She glanced at him, but didn't say hello. That was odd. When the mayor walked in, Gil knew something was wrong.

There were a few people browsing and he didn't want a scene in his store.

'What's up?' He smiled at them both, even though he knew it couldn't be good news.

The mayor didn't look at him as he walked over to the till. 'I've heard some unsettling news. I've been trying to call you all morning.'

'It's been busy in here. I left my cell phone upstairs.' That's where he hoped it was anyway. Hopefully it was in yesterday's pants, which were still on the living room floor from last night. She'd been there when he'd woken up in the morning, but she'd slipped out with a kiss before the sun had even peeked above the hills. He drunk his coffee with a grin as he'd watched the sunrise. He tried hard not to smile about it in front of the mayor. 'You could've called the store line.'

The mayor stared at him as though Gil was supposed know what was going on. Gil stared back. He knew exactly what this was about. Someone had seen Jasmine leave this morning—or had they seen them eating dinner and leaving restraint like an ordinary happy couple? That someone had obviously told the mayor exactly who Jasmine was.

The mayor huffed and lowered his voice. 'It might be a good idea for you to step down from the festival committee. You seem to have got your interests conflicted.'

The mayor seemed to have got his panties twisted. 'I've been making sure that the TV show does a good job on the River Man, just like you told me to.' He widened his grin.

The mayor's eyelid twitched. 'I know your history with that girl and I know she doesn't give a damn about this town.'

'This town never gave a damn about her either, but they're here to do their job. They're professionals.' Who were thinking that the mayor's precious monster was more human than anyone knew.

It could be anyone. Gil exhaled.

The River Man could literally be anyone in town. Anyone with a vested interest in keeping the myth alive. But why so many deer kills over the last ten years? There was no need. People already knew the legend, and around here the murder from twenty years ago was still considered fresh.

'Their job was to talk about the festival, not pull apart our River Man. How deep are they digging?'

He knew he should tell the mayor that it might be called a hoax, but the words didn't form. The mayor wanted him off the committee so he didn't need to say anything, that must be that conflict of interest. 'No idea. I was too busy to ask.'

Nancy hovered not far behind the mayor now. She managed to look both concerned and scandalised. 'We didn't want to do this to you, but you left us no choice. We can't have the committee associated with those people.'

Gil looked at her. 'Those people? What, the TV show that you were so happy to have here?'

'You know who I mean,' Nancy said. 'You should be thinking about yourself. You don't need that trouble. Your grandfather would be appalled.'

Gil laughed. His grandfather would be thrilled with the disruption to those who thought they ran the town. He wished the old man was still here. He'd know a few River Man tales.

'This is serious, son,' the mayor said. 'You are either on the committee and keeping away from her, or you are—'

'I got it. Pick a side.' He shouldn't be having to pick sides. They were on the same side. The mayor should be wanting to find out the truth. Unless he already knew. 'Without me, I doubt the crew will talk freely to the committee.'

The mayor hesitated. 'Well, they can talk to Nancy if they need anything.'

'I'll let Jasmine know.' Gil said coolly. He hoped that they had everything they needed, because he doubted the committee would be helpful now they knew who Jasmine was. They'd scuttle their five minutes of TV fame because of her. He saw how deep the hatred ran; it was no wonder she'd left and not looked back. It was a shame the people his age had been fed the same poison and would no doubt feed it to their kids without ever knowing why. Why were the Royles and Thorpes so hated?

The mayor turned to leave. Which was a good thing as there were now a couple of customers waiting to be served, pretending that they weren't listening to every word.

Gil couldn't resist one last strike. 'You know, I didn't believe her when she said people here don't forgive or forget. Guess she was right. I was hoping she'd be wrong.'

The mayor broke step but didn't turn. Nancy followed him out like an obedient dog. Now he wasn't on the committee, he had a whole lot more free time. Guess they wouldn't be inviting him back next year either.

Or the year after.

He was now one of *those* people.

# Chapter 8

The ranger was a middle-aged man, who'd taken his hat off and rubbed his hair so many times it looked like he'd rubbed the front half of his hair off. Jasmine sipped her coffee. Living in Seattle, she'd become a bit of a coffee snob. She liked the expensive stuff, simply because she could afford it and she'd gone without for so long.

The best part of meeting the ranger was Simon wasn't a local. He wasn't bound up by generations of talk and local lore. 'Do you have any photos of the deer kills?'

'I can do better. I kept the deer.'

She almost dropped her coffee. 'What?'

She'd been told it had been destroyed. Did the mayor know that the ranger had kept the deer and then lied to her? Or was Simon acting alone?

'I knew you people were coming and I wanted you to see it. But this has to be off the show. You can't tell anyone I have it because everyone wanted it gone. They like to pretend these things aren't happening.'

'Where is it?' Hopefully in a freezer, but from the look on Simon's face that wasn't going to be the answer.

'Out the back. It's a bit ripe.'

It would be after sitting around for a few days. But she was okay with dead things and the bugs that liked to colonise them. 'That's okay. What will you do with it once I've had a look?'

She wished he'd spoken to her sooner, but maybe that would've looked suspicious and he was already wary, insisting nothing was recorded.

'Bury it like I was supposed to. I had dug the hole and everything.'

She'd seen the pictures Gil had taken, but he hadn't been taking them with a scientific eye. 'Did it look like a bear attack to you?'

A bear was one of the theories that had been floated, even though the creature was called the River Man. Lumbering gait had come up a few times, and he was heavy set. Both of which matched up with what she remembered. She was keen to eliminate things from the list of possibilities.

Posing logical suggestions and then discounting them made for good TV, it allowed people to think about it at home.

Simon shook his head. 'I've seen bear attacks. This was no bear.'

The carcass was probably so contaminated it wouldn't be worth getting samples. 'You didn't happen to take any swabs or tissue samples?'

Simon shook his head. 'If they knew I had the carcass, they'd find a way to run me out of town.'

She didn't doubt that at all. Conform or get out seemed to be the way they liked it in Bitterwood. 'I appreciate what you've done.'

'I'd appreciate it if you could find out who's behind this.'

'Who?' Her eyebrows lifted. Simon seemed pretty sure that a human was behind the deaths. Part of her knew that made the most sense too, but she didn't want to believe it. The hoax had been running for too long.

'Don't tell me you believe this River Man nonsense? There's some sick bastard out there killing deer and it's only a matter of time until he kills a person.'

'The River Man *has* killed people.' There were several deaths attributed to the legend, stretching back a hundred years.

The ranger shook his head. 'I know they think he has. But I think some of them can be chalked up to misadventure.' He drained his coffee. 'When I first moved up here, I took an interest in the local legend. I wanted to see if I could find it. Fancied myself an amateur sleuth. I read up on those murders. You know the whole heart missing thing only started twenty years ago with that last fellow. Before that it was just death by cuts.'

'Fascinating.' She wasn't even faking it. She downed the rest of her coffee. Simon could be full of all kinds of interesting facts. 'Probably should have had that after looking at the carcass, not before.'

'I have whisky for after that. You'll need it.'

He had no idea how strong her stomach was, but she smiled anyway. 'I like the way you think.'

He beamed. 'You know what I said about sleuthing?'

'Yes.' What other surprises did he have for her? Her heart gave a flip. She could actually be talking to the man posing as the River Man—Simon did know rather a lot about the creature's habits. And no one knew who the killer was, or if there was a killer at all. As Simon had said, misadventure could explain most of the deaths. But peoples' hearts didn't just fall out by themselves. That was a new twist.

She glanced at Simon. No, he wasn't local. He had no ties and no reason to kill. But then, no one came to Bitterwood for fun. Had he been coming here for the last twenty years before finally getting a job? If she was looking for a killer, she couldn't rule out anyone. Simon's insistence that nothing be recorded and his name be kept out of the show cast another shadow of doubt. If he was an amateur sleuth, wouldn't he want his moment in the spotlight?

'Well, I set up some cameras at the most popular sites.' Simon beamed as though expecting a reward.

'Oh my God, you have footage!' She could've kissed him.

He seemed to get as excited as her. 'I've been wanting to share this for so long. And I didn't know who to trust. If I can't trust *Cryptid or Hoax?* who can I trust?'

Her apprehension settled. He was just a ranger who was filling in his spare time looking into cryptids. 'You a fan of the show?'

'A little.' Red crept over his cheeks. He wasn't just a little fan.

'I might have a spare hat or T-shirt at the motel.'

He walked over to his desk and pulled a thumb drive out of the drawer. 'This is from the evening the deer was killed.'

'Can I use it in the show?'

'Only if you don't say where it came from.'

'I can do that.' She wanted to shove it into the computer and check out the footage now, but she settled herself. Corpse first. 'Let's look at the deer.'

Out the back turned out to be a half-hour hike. The digger sat by the hole ready to bury the deer. As they got closer, she didn't see the deer. Her steps slowed. 'Where is it?'

'It's in the hole.'

She glanced at the ranger, then pulled out her phone to take some pictures.

'I'll just let the guys know that I'm going to be late.' And where she was, just in case she ended up in the hole with the deer.

\*\*\*


Gil closed the shop at lunchtime. He didn't usually, he just ate his lunch when he could and got on with it. He didn't want to get on with it today. He was still fuming that the mayor had come into *his* shop and told him how to behave, like he was some schoolkid.

Was Bitterwood really that shallow? Were the people he had called friends so desperate to maintain their moral high ground that they didn't care if people changed.

Maybe they were jealous that Jasmine had left and returned a success, proving them all wrong and reminding everyone that people can change. A smile twisted his lips. Yeah, maybe it was those who didn't change who were the real worry.

As he walked through the town, there were plenty of people he didn't recognise, those who were just here for the festival. It was a nice feeling not to know everyone, something he hadn't paid attention to in previous years. The centre of town was being transformed with the stage for music and the stalls along the streets, now closed to traffic. He kept going and noticed that when he smiled at people he knew, they weren't exactly welcoming. If they did smile, it was brief before they suddenly found something else to occupy their attention.

News really did travel fast.

Had the mayor expected him to tuck tail and obey?

That was exactly what had been expected of him. For the first time in his life he wasn't one of them. He was the kind of person that didn't get a warm welcome and who was treated with suspicion. How long it would last he had no idea. Until the TV show left?

Oh God, and when they proclaimed the River Man a hoax?

He stopped and looked back at the town centre filled with much-needed tourists and their dollars. They would all blame him. He'd be the only one here to blame and they would want a scapegoat. Jasmine had warned him she'd be leaving, and he'd be left to pick up the pieces. He was just starting to see what those pieces looked like. Had the committee known all along that having the show here would bring no good? Or had this been a convenient way of casting blame aside if having the show went badly?

If the River Man was a hoax, someone must know. That kind of thing would be hard to keep a secret. Surely the mayor would know it couldn't be real. Was it a publicity stunt to grow the festival, thus the extra deer deaths? But then why agree to letting the TV show come?

Did his father know who was killing the deer? As Chief of Police, he should at the very least have an idea. Gil was very tempted to go to the police station and find out. But he didn't. He made his way to where the TV crew were doing interviews with locals. They had whittled yesterday's line down to half a dozen.

The locals were talking about what they'd seen as though it was real. They'd end up looking like fools when, if, the hoax, was proven. Who would gain by keeping the hoax going?

From where he was standing, it looked like the whole town had a vested interest in the hoax.

His truck rolled down the street and then parked near the motel. Jasmine bounced out the truck, clutching something in her hand.

She startled when she saw him, then grinned. 'Did you need your keys back?'

'I'm good. Just stretching my legs on my lunchbreak. I thought I'd see what was going on.' He nodded at where the interviews were now being recorded.

'They'll almost be done. They started at the river this morning. Vary the locations and try to keep it all relaxed and natural and all that.'

It was all fake. They had picked these people out because they would sound good on the show or their story was interesting. 'I got kicked off the committee. I don't know how much help I'm going to be to you now.'

In his gut he was worried she'd only been with him to get good info. Keep him on side and all of that. He'd picked her over the place he lived. What if everyone shunned him until he left town? A little part of him died. This was his home. His life.

But he refused to be told how to behave. There was indignation simmering that the mayor thought he could force him into line. How had the mayor sent word around so fast? Was it everyone or just some? It felt like everyone.

He knew it couldn't be.

'What? Why? Oh...' She frowned as she realised. 'Me? Really?'

'It's the only thing I can think of. I did get a warning from my father before the visit from the mayor.'

She shook her head. 'You're an adult and they're trying to run your life?'

He was beginning to see that was how things really worked here. Those who played the game got rewarded and those who didn't got ignored. Guess the mayor would stop asking when he'd be nominating for the town council. If the reward for staying in line was more rules to follow, he wasn't sure he wanted to play. But if he wanted to live and do business here, he couldn't burn his bridges the way Jasmine had done.

Had been a little too rash in telling the mayor to get stuffed? Even if he had been, he wasn't going to go back and beg for forgiveness. He'd done nothing wrong.

He shrugged as though it meant nothing. The wound was just starting to sting. 'Some people can really hold a grudge.'

'One that goes back generations, apparently. My family aren't the only ones scraping by and yet we were always the ones getting in trouble.' She sighed and shook her head. 'So how does it feel to be shoved off your high horse?'

'My high horse?'

'You know, the one all the righteous folk ride around here. Guess you have to walk like the rest of us.' She grinned.

She was teasing, but she was also speaking the truth. This was what it was like to be on the out with the people who ran the town. Even when he'd left home he hadn't been cast aside. But back then his grandfather had stood up for him. This time he had no one. His father would gloat.

The guys started to wrap up the interview they were doing.

'Gil, you know how I said I thought it was a hoax? Well, now I'm damn sure. They threw you off the committee because you were helping me too much. Is it possible they know?'

'No...' They couldn't. 'That kind of thing can't be kept secret. Not for a century. What makes you so sure?'

She pressed her lips together and for a moment he saw the distrust on her face. She wasn't sure which side he was on.

'I want to know the truth. If someone here knows, they're protecting a murderer.' Assuming the deer deaths were committed by the same person who killed the hunter over twenty years ago.

'And deer mutilator. The most recent one was killed by a human.' She glanced at the guys. 'You need to be sure that you want in, because if there is a leak from what we discuss, I'll know it's you.'

'I have to get back to work. But if you want me to poke around I can. I'm sure there's a few people who will talk to me.'

'I'll let you know.' She grabbed his hand. 'Be careful. He could be anyone.'

Gil drew in a breath and nodded. 'You shouldn't have gone to the ranger's alone. I can't believe they let you.' He inclined his head at her colleagues.

She shrugged. 'Some people don't want to be on camera, and I respect that. Besides, I let them know where I was. I can't assume that everyone is a monster.'

'Whatever you find, you will have to turn over to the police.' There was a killer and people keeping the secret.

'That's worked real well, hasn't it?' Her eyes widened. 'Sorry, I know he's your father. Besides, we don't have anything yet. Please don't tell your father. If we go public too soon this town will close up faster than a clam.'

Gil couldn't help but smile, but he was worried that someone in power knew exactly what was going on. He didn't want to dwell on what would happen when the crew tipped their hand, but he was guessing that it wouldn't end well.

*** 

Jasmine played the footage from the ranger's camera for Luke and Cal. She wanted to show it to Gil, but part of her still expected him to run back across the road to the safe side of Bitterwood. If he got in too deep with the crew and what they were uncovering, he'd never be able to do that. And she couldn't do that to him.

On the screen, the creature lumbered out of the scrub. In the twilight it was hard to see much detail; it dragged the deer behind it. Happy with the location, the River Man paused to put its hands on its hips and catch its breath. A very human gesture. Then it went to wipe its face and it lifted its face off.

'Damn. Did you see that?' Luke whispered.

'Yeah. Pity we couldn't see his face.' Jasmine paused the recording. 'Well, I think we have a confirmed hoax.'

Cal nodded. 'Yeah, and that dude's been killing deer. Maybe even people.'

'He doesn't know that we know,' Luke said.

'Yet.' Jasmine was well aware of the risk once this information got out. 'Someone in town has to know who this is.'

'Is that all we have?' Cal turned to look at her. 'The ranger could have set this up.'

'He's a wannabe cryptid hunter. He got curious about all the dead deer and set up cameras. No one knows about them except him.' And the minute whoever was behind this knew the cameras were there, Simon would also be a target.

'Are they still up?'

'Yeah. I looked at the deer and Simon gave me his notes on the other ones that have been found. Killed with a bullet, then cut up to mask the bullet-entry wound—but Simon knew what he was looking for. Wanna bet the bullet is in the heart?'

'Do I look stupid?' Luke raised his eyebrows.

Jasmine smiled. 'Do I have to answer that?'

'Okay, so we have a dude in a River Man costume shooting deer and then dumping the bodies, minus the heart. But he's only doing it every couple of years? Why?' Cal was frowning.

'Keep people afraid?' Jasmine knew that wasn't enough. 'But that doesn't explain the historical data. There were three River Man deaths in the early nineteen-hundreds. Then nothing until sixty-three.'

'And how many dead deer?' Cal was drawing up a timeline on a notepad.

'No idea ... certainly none while I lived here, that I know of. Deer aren't light. We're looking for a fit man, who can hunt.' That he'd dressed up to dump the carcass was impressive. It would have been far easier out of character ... probably easier to explain too. Although he'd waited until dusk when people would be heading home, the location was far enough away from the town that there wouldn't be any casual observers. She'd stood there only days ago.

'Or his accomplice can hunt,' Luke said. 'How many people know?'

'Can't be many.'

'That's probably the way they like it. I want to talk to the hunter again. The one whose buddy was murdered. I think we can safely say that he wasn't taken by the River Man.' Cal tapped the pen. 'Let's call it a re-enactment. Go to the same spot and all that.'

'Okay ... but what are we really doing?'

'Seeing what could be seen.' Cal pointed at the screen. 'That's a lot of effort to go to just for kicks.'

Jasmine shook her head. 'Not if the sole purpose is to keep the festival alive and exciting. Money is a good motivator.'

'You got no clues, Jas. You saw it?' Luke stared at her as though he was daring her to lie.

She closed her eyes and saw it fighting with her uncle. Not fighting. It had to have been a suit. Was her uncle helping the killer get undressed?

Her uncle would never let a film crew on his property. He'd never give an interview either. But she could go and see him, give him a chance to tell her what happened that night. 'If we are going to do this re-enactment we're going to need to scramble. And I still need to go and film a few sciency bits.'

'Is it worth it? What angle are we going to take?' Luke wasn't looking convinced about the re-enactment.

'We've uncovered a long-running hoax, that has to be worth some ratings. We haven't done that before.' Cal grinned.

'We cover all bases and hand it over to Becca.' Their producer was going to be thrilled. 'We should probably let her know what's going on anyway. She still thinks it's a cryptid.'

'She's going to tell us to go to the cops.' Luke said. 'We should go to the cops.'

'And we will when we have enough to force him to act. He was chief when that hunter was killed and he's done nothing to find the deer mutilator.'

'Can't imagine he's going to be thrilled when we break the case and prove his incompetence.' Cal drew something else on the notepad then crossed it out. 'Maybe we should lie and call it a cryptid. Once we're out of town we can call up the chief.'

'You scared the River Man will get you.' Luke waggled his fingers at Cal.

'No.' Cal pointed at the screen. 'I'm worried he will.'

# Chapter 9

Gil checked before he opened his door; he didn't want another confrontation with the mayor or his father. Jasmine was standing there with two pizzas. He opened up and let her in. 'You done already?'

She nodded. 'For today. The camera crew will be filming the festival tomorrow. Luke will do his bit then.'

'And what is he going to say?' Were they going to call it out as a hoax?

'That it's a hoax. An elaborate hoax for sure. But we can't lie.' She gave him a quick kiss as she brushed past him. 'The producer wants us to bring in the cops and tell the mayor. There'll be a big meeting tomorrow.'

Which he wouldn't be invited to now he wasn't on the committee. 'Dad won't like that.'

'I know. He should have called it out as a hoax years ago. Gil, is it possible he knows?' She put the pizza on the coffee table and took off her shoes.

The word 'no' formed on his lips, but didn't get any further. How else could his father's lack of interest in River Man-related crime be explained? 'I don't know. But why would he protect the person if he knew?'

'Money, for the town ... I mean look at how many people have shown up for the weekend. It was never this big when we were at school.'

'What if the town were paying someone to keep the myth alive?' He didn't want to think that his dad was corrupt. After the effort his father had made to make sure that Gil had never strayed from what was expected...

He poured two glasses of wine and handed her one. She was going to walk away soon and he'd be left doing the damage control.

She took a sip. 'That is also a possibility.'

'Has anything like this ever happened before?'

'Nope. I hope it never happens again. Because of the unsolved murder this may never get to air. Time and money for nothing.'

'Is that all you care about?' The girl he'd known wouldn't have cared. Or would she? Had she kept her secrets even back then? How well did he really know her? Once she'd been forbidden, the bad girl that guys like him shouldn't go near. Now it didn't matter.

Nothing they did mattered. In two days, this was done. This time he was going to have to get over her and move on. He should have never got hung up on her. It was clear she was never going to put down roots. She would always be on the move. He wasn't like that. He needed a place to call home. He couldn't imagine being a wanderer.

'It's what I have to care about. TV shows aren't cheap to make. There are so many people involved. The cost of travel, the equipment ... If we can't do this episode then we have to find something else to replace it. But the mayor was keen on us being here.'

'I think he was hoping for less truth and more fluff. I wish I could be there for the meeting tomorrow.' He'd love to be able to see the mayor's face. His father's too.

'It's probably better that you aren't.'

He knew what she meant, but it was hard to put distance between himself and what was happening when Jasmine was on his sofa, leaning against him.

'Enough talk about that, let's eat the pizza before the grease cools.' She flipped open the lid and pulled out a piece that didn't want to leave the other slices from the amount of cheese that stretched between them.

'So what do you want to talk about?' Maybe they only had the River Man and the past. That thought carved a hole in his chest. Somehow he'd been thinking this was more than what it was. He'd confused excitement with lust. She always raised his pulse and made him want to stretch his wings. This time he might have already jumped without checking to see if he'd be able to land safely.

How was he going to put his life back together?

He'd managed last time. Maybe she swept in and changed people for the better without realising the effect she had on people.

'Anything else. People talk about stuff. Who's going to win the game between the cops and firemen this year?'

'Firemen without a doubt.' And he wasn't saying that just because he was a volunteer firefighter.

'You are so biased,' she said between bites.

'Will you be around to watch the game?' Not that his baseball skills were anything to write home about, but he could hold his own in the annual game, assuming he was still allowed to play. What was this, third grade?

'Should be.' Smiled and sank her teeth into the pizza. 'So aside from baseball and firefighting, what else do you get up to?'

'Hiking, bit of fishing. Shop keeps me pretty busy though.' He had a teenager help out on the weekends, but even then he didn't trust the store entirely to another.

'Have you had a holiday since your grandfather died?'

'No.' Until now he hadn't really thought about it. Where would he go? What would he do? But there was a whole lot of world out there waiting to be explored. While he was tied to the shop and the town, he was never going anywhere. The walls of his carefully built life moved closer. They had been moving closer for years and he hadn't noticed because it had been so gradual. Is that what happened around here? The prison snuck up on you until one day you looked up and found yourself trapped. 'I don't know if there's anywhere I'd want to go.'

'What about the beach? California sunshine? Or skiing? Or New York City with all its bustle? The Grand Canyon.' As she spoke, her eyes lit up.

'Have you been to all those places?' How could she even come back here where she had been everywhere?

'Yeah, I travel all the time.' She sighed and sipped her wine. 'Sometimes there's nothing better than getting back to Tricia's and doing nothing for a week except watch TV and lie on the sofa. I need to think about what I'm going to do when the show ends.'

'Like teach?'

She laughed, her body shaking next to his. 'Noooo. Research maybe.'

'When you left, how'd you get to Seattle?'

'Hitched. I didn't want to waste the money your father threw at me.'

'You are so lucky to be alive.' He wouldn't have been brave enough to hitch to Seattle back then. He wasn't sure he'd do it now.

'Not everyone is a killer looking for prey. In nature it's easy to tell, but humans still have their tells.'

They were circling back to the dangerous talk of who the River Man might be. He didn't want to be looking at everyone in town though suspicion-tinted glasses. These were people that he'd known all of his life. His neighbours, his friends, his customers. Right now all of them were giving him the less than subtle cold shoulder. If he didn't correct his course, it would become permanent.

When Jasmine left, all the fuss would all die down. When a pebble was thrown into the river there was a splash and a few ripples and then nothing. After a few months it would be like she'd never been here. Not a single ripple would remain. He didn't want that. He didn't want his life to go back to how it had been. She was here to wake him up. Just like last time.

He smiled at her. She was his guardian angel come to kick him in the butt and do something with his life. He had no idea what though.

He picked up a piece of pizza. 'You finished school in Seattle and got good enough grades to get into college?'

'I always had good grades, Gil. But the teachers were never going to give me an award or even a certificate. I knew that finishing school and doing were well was my way out. Tricia said that every time she came home. I wanted to be like her. Free. I never wanted to be like my mother. Trapped.' She pressed her lips together. Her gaze somewhere in the distance. A memory that he couldn't see.

'Is that how you see me? Trapped?'

She turned her head. For a moment she didn't answer. Then he didn't want her to answer and confirm his fears. He was trapped. He'd missed the chance to break free and now he was part of the town and the town was part of him. He'd never worried about that before.

He'd been content. Why did she make him feel like he was missing out?

Was he?

Jasmine put down her glass and moved so that she was kneeling over him. 'I don't think you are trapped. You can leave anytime you want. The cage door is open. I don't think you have ever been hungry enough to want to leave.'

He was the fat house cat and she was the lean tiger.

She kissed him. Her lips warm against his. She tasted like red wine and pepperoni. His hands found her hips. It was going to hurt when she left. Hurt worse than the first time. He doubted she'd be back again.

'I shouldn't want you. I know you're only temporary. The dream I can't hold on to when I wake.' Jasmine would always be the one who got away.

Unless he chased her.

Could one ever tame a tiger? He didn't think so, and caging her would be cruel. All he could do was make the most of the time they had.

She smiled; her fingertips brushed his cheek. 'I always knew you'd never be mine. But that never stopped me from dreaming.'

'We should dream harder, or more often.'

'That would mean sleeping through life. That wouldn't work either.'

She was too damn practical. Did she treat all of her lovers so casually? He didn't want to ask and get the stats. He didn't need to know. But he doubted many got a second chance.

She toyed with the buttons on his shirt before flicking one open. 'Did you want me to stay tonight?'

People had seen her arrive and he had no doubt they'd note what time she would leave. The damage was already done.

'Stay. Let's not waste what's left.' His hand slid under her shirt to brush the warm skin of her waist.

Glass shattered and Gil froze.

Jasmine did too. Her head tilted to the side. Another window broke and this time the alarm went off. That wasn't across the street, that was downstairs. His shop.

She was already moving, grabbing her shoes and getting ready to run down into whatever trouble was waiting.

He picked up the phone and called the police—which he really hated doing. He glanced at Jasmine. First her SUV, now this. Maybe it wasn't related or maybe someone wanted her out of town real bad.

Or someone was worried that the crew would get too close to the truth.

With the cops on their way, Gil grabbed a heavy flashlight. 'You can wait here.'

Jasmine shook her head. 'And leave you alone?'

Together they went downstairs. Jasmine had her phone held up, recording whatever was down there. The front of the shop had been sprayed with a big green RM.

'Didn't think the River Man was into graffiti,' Jasmine said.

Both of the front windows had been smashed in. Gil opened up the door and shut off the alarm. His neighbours were already coming out to see what the fuss was about. They glanced at the damage and made noises about bad luck and then they saw Jasmine recording everything on her phone.

A few looked puzzled, but it didn't last for long as they were informed about who she was, then a look of knowing crossed their face. Jasmine's slow circle came to a stop. Gil glanced over at who she was looking at, but he didn't see anyone.

Some of the people staring he didn't know. They were probably out-of-towners. Some people rented out their spare rooms to make some extra money over this weekend. He didn't think the damage was done by a stranger. It was only his shop, not the whole street.

Then his father and another cop were pushing through the onlookers.

His heart sank. His father did that quick assessing gaze that Gil was well used to, before his face hardened when he saw Jasmine. Gil made his way to her, reaching her side before his father.

'Hang around with trash and that's what you attract.' His father put his hands on his hips and glared at Jasmine. 'You still bring trouble wherever you go.'

\*\*\*

Jasmine looked at the chief. Maybe he wasn't aware she was still recording. She'd lowered her phone to her side when he'd appeared. 'Easier to blame the victim than find the vandal?'

She knew she was poking her finger into the beehive, but she was done with dancing around. 'If someone is trying to hurt me or run me out of town, shouldn't you be trying to find out who? It wouldn't look good on the TV if we had to mention being run out of town by biased locals who couldn't stand that the girl they loved to hate had turned her life around and found success.'

'Wouldn't look too good if your past was leaked.' The chief levelled his gaze at her.

'What about yours? What kind of a man threatens a sixteen-year-old girl?' Gil said it loud enough for the closest of the eavesdroppers to hear.

Jasmine gave his hand a squeeze. He didn't need to defend her. He still had to live with these people. 'I'll be gone in a few days. Then you can go back to hating me and my family for having the nerve to be poor. Right now you'd better ask for witnesses. Maybe someone saw something, or perhaps there are some cameras?'

'Don't tell me how to do my job. With me, son.' The chief went into the shop and Gil reluctantly followed.

Jasmine was sure that his father was about to try and tell Gil off. This vandalism would be written off as something random, even though everyone knew that it wasn't. She stopped the recording and watched the footage. She hadn't imagined it. Her cousin had been there for just a moment before leaving.

The other officer walked up to her. A young guy, she'd probably gone to school with him, but she couldn't remember his name. His badge said Tanner. There had been a few Tanner boys at school, all related somehow.

He swallowed. 'Can I ask you a few questions?'

'Sure.' She'd do her bit.

'Where were you at the time of the incident?'

'Upstairs with Gil, we were having dinner.' Someone had known where she'd be. Maybe this wasn't about her and it was about Gil. He was the one walking out of step and not behaving properly.

They'd thrown him off the committee in the hope that he'd stop seeing her. They couldn't even let him have a few days of fun.

'And then what happened?'

'And then we heard glass break, twice, the alarm went off and we came down to see what was going on. And here we are.'

'That's it?'

'That's it.' She smiled.

'Do you or Gil have any enemies?'

'Are you joking?' Did he not know who she was? 'When I lived here, I was Jasmine Thorpe. Half the town hated me because of my surname.'

He glanced up from his notepad. A smile formed. 'Did you date my brother?'

She wouldn't have called it dating, and she couldn't remember which Tanner boy it had been. 'Possibly.'

The Tanners were somewhere closer to respectable than she had been, but not so high that messing with her would get them into trouble. Judging by his uniform, they were working their way up the Bitterwood social ladder.

The cop glanced at the spray paint. 'Doesn't seem like what someone would write if they were threatening you.'

She shrugged. 'I am looking into the creature.' She gave him another smile. 'What do you think? Myth, hoax or cryptid?'

He shook his head. 'I stick to the facts.'

'And what do they tell you?'

He stared at her for a moment. 'That people will blame anything out of the ordinary on the River Man. I doubt very much that he did this though. Too far from the river for a start.'

'I agree. So do you all draw straws to see who gets stuck with the dead deer?'

'No.' He shook his head with a laugh. 'Chief usually has a quick look before it gets destroyed.'

'So no one looks into it?'

Tanner frowned. 'No, it's just a deer.'

'But there's been a few of them, all killed the same way, apparently. Don't serial killers start with animals?'

'Serial killer? This is Bitterwood. We don't have serial killers. Worst thing we get is a few break-ins. Maybe a fight ... what have you found out?'

'It's my job to ask questions and put together a show. But the dead deer have been bugging me. Animals don't just take hearts and they kill more frequently.' She paused, as though only just thinking of it. 'Have there been any other animal mutilations?'

Tanner tilted his head. 'Don Sander's cow. It was killed and was in a real mess when found. People blamed the River Man, but it could have been anything.'

'So you don't think it's real?'

'Nah.' He shook his head.

'Then who killed that hunter twenty years ago?' She knew he wouldn't have been much older than her when it had happened but there had to be office gossip.

He paused before answering. 'Er ... we don't know.'

'No suspects?'

'Not that I know of.' He was getting wary now. 'I think I should be the one asking the questions.'

Jasmine shrugged. 'Okay. What do you need to know?'

'Um ... Does the TV show have any enemies?'

'Ask the person who slashed our SUV tires. This seems to fit their style.'

Tanner's mouth hung open for a moment before he shut it. 'That would imply that someone doesn't want you here.'

Jasmine smiled. 'Exactly. And the person feeding the River Man myth has the most to lose.'

Tanner blinked a couple of times then stepped back. 'I should go and find the chief.'

'You do that. If you want me, you know where to find me.'

'Here ... or at the motel?'

But she'd already turned around and started walking toward the shop.

*** 

Gil watched his father cast a quick look over the broken glass and the two rocks sitting on the shop floor. He knew his father wouldn't do anything. 'So are you going to increase patrols to stop this behaviour during the festival?'

'It was only your shop. Why would that be?'

'They wanted hardware and we interrupted the theft?'

'Gil, be sensible. The first person I see when I get here is her. Everyone knows you and her are—'

'Jasmine. Jasmine and I are old friends who are catching up. And it shouldn't matter what I do or with who. My store has been damaged and I'll need to put in an insurance claim. I'll need a police report number.'

'I'll give you that. But you need to understand that you have provoked some people.' His father put his hands on his hips.

'Some people need to stop worrying about what I do and pay more attention to the laws they are breaking. Are you even going to investigate?'

'Can't get fingerprints off a rock and I know you don't have any cameras.'

That would be the next thing that he did. He'd put up cameras. He'd been meaning to, but it had never been important. Bitterwood was usually safe.

'I heard you got thrown off the committee. That girl is ruining your life. Again.' His father nodded as though expecting Gil to join in and agree.

'Gossip does move fast. Their bias is showing ... if the mayor can't treat all the people in his town equally then maybe he should be the one being forced out.'

His father opened his mouth to argue, but stopped.

Jasmine walked into the shop. 'Need some help cleaning and boarding up the windows?'

'You've done enough, don't you think?' His father snapped.

Jasmine didn't flinch or cower at his father's tone. 'You know, I've meaning to thank you for what you did ten years ago. Why, if you hadn't have given me that fifty and told me to get lost, I might never have left this place. The world is so much bigger than Bitterwood. And the people are so much nicer. Not hung up on decades-old grudges. You did me a favour, Chief. If not for you I might have stayed, now look at me. I'm on TV and people listen to me. They care about me.' Her tone was pure sugar, and she was even smiling.

His father's face darkened as her words struck home.

'Why don't you get a broom from out the back, Jas?' Gil cut in. He didn't want his father to lose his temper and he didn't want Jasmine being caught in the storm. They only had a few more days and he didn't want to waste them talking about what an asshole his father could be.

'Sure thing. You finished taking photos? Gathering evidence? Or were you just going to brush over this the way you do the mutilated deer?'

'You're interfering in a police investigation. I can have you locked up,' his father snarled.

'What investigation? If you lock me up, how long do you think it will take the station to get their lawyers involved?' She took a step forward. 'You can't bully me anymore. And if you take it out on my family I will hear about. I can get them good lawyers too.' She glanced at him. 'Anything else you need from the cupboard?'

'Not right now.' He'd never seen Jasmine act so defiant. No one ever stood up to his father. Moving out of home had been his big act of defiance. Since then he'd barely spoken to his father. They'd talked more over the last couple of days than they had in years. He tossed her the key and she caught it one-handed.

Jasmine gave him a nod and disappeared down aisle two. She'd find the storeroom. There wasn't that much down there.

'Did you hear the way she talked to me?'

Gil stared at his father. 'She's right. If you're done, I'm going to secure my shop. I'll be calling my insurance company in the morning so send me that police report number by email.'

'This won't end well, Gil. You got away with it last time because you were young.'

'Really?' Gil crossed his arms. 'What exactly do you want from me? To follow some coded set of behaviour? To only associate with certain pre-approved people? Do you realise how ridiculous that sounds?'

'You are an Easton. We were one of the founders.'

'And you know who else was one of the founders? The Royles. I went and spoke to Mrs Harrison at the library. She showed me all kinds of interesting things about the start of the town. So how come we ended up on the right side of the law and they ended up on the wrong side?' Gil saw Jasmine lingering in the shadows; was she waiting for his father to leave, or listening? He would've told her what he'd found if they hadn't been interrupted.

The other cop walked in. 'I've spoken to a few of the onlookers. No one saw anything.'

'Put that in your report. It was probably out-of-towners looking to steal hardware or camping supplies. They must have been interrupted.' His father parroted what Gil had suggested.

'And the RM tag?' The young cop looked a little concerned. Maybe he still wanted to do his job properly. Good for him. Give it another few years and that would probably wear off. Or he'd be told to toe the line and not make trouble if he wanted that promotion.

'Kids ... who knows when that happened. I'm sure Gil can get it cleaned off. Right, son?'

'Yeah.'

The young cop looked at both of them and decided that it wasn't worth stepping any deeper into what was obviously a family dispute in progress.

'Okay, I'll leave you to it.' Tanner took a step back. 'I'll wait outside for you, Chief.'

'I'm leaving. Nothing more to do here.'

Gil didn't say anything. He wanted his father out of his shop and out of his life.

# Chapter 10

Jasmine hadn't stayed the night even though she'd wanted to. By the time the windows had been boarded up and the glass swept up, neither of them had felt like doing much. Gil had told her about his trip to the library—some people were still willing to damage their reputation and talk to him. She was really hoping that this public shunning was only temporary and once she left everyone would welcome him back with open arms.

The roads were quiet as she headed through town in the new rental vehicle. Today they would film some of the festival and get the mayor to say his piece. But first there was a meeting with the Chief of Police and the mayor to discuss the hoax. Cal was going to paint it as a really interesting discovery. A long-running hoax that had been so believable only modern investigative techniques had uncovered the truth.

They were trying to dress a pig in a prom dress and crown her queen.

She was expecting to have to fold the whole episode up and write off the week's work. No one who lived in Bitterwood was going to want to hear that their creature was a hoax even though they had the footage to prove it.

They didn't know who it was in the River Man suit.

However her uncle did. She'd told the guys she was going to see her family this morning, but what she really wanted was to get her uncle's tale and see what he knew. If they could find out who it was in the suit, they could really stick it to Chief Easton. It would also reveal how inept he was.

She passed her mother's house and went further down the road to her uncle's place. The ever-changing field of car bodies was still there in various states of repair or dismemberment. He was always able to get parts and knew how to fix everything.

She parked the car. Dogs started barking and two raced toward the car. Jasmine let them bark and carry on before slowly nudging open the door.

These dogs wouldn't know her, and they didn't look too friendly either.

Between the two properties there was now a fence—to keep the dogs in or to stop kids from wandering across? Playing hide and seek in the cars probably hadn't been the safest game, but it had been fun. Even back then she'd known that she was never going to get the pretty dolls that other kids had.

Her cousin came out of the house in track pants and called off the dogs. They raced back to the porch lured by whatever meat Theo had in his hand. He dropped it into the bowls and the two dogs snapped and snarled at each other, arguing about who got what juicy bit. Blood clung to their muzzles.

These weren't pets like her uncle had kept. These were guard dogs.

She glanced at Theo. He was grinning. He'd been grinning last night. A chill cut through her and settled in her bones. Maybe she shouldn't have come here alone. However, if she'd brought a crew or one of the guys, her uncle would've never talked.

This was her family and she had to deal with them.

She smiled and shut the door, but she didn't lock it.

'What are you doing all this way out here?' Theo called.

'Came to see Bert. He up?'

'Yeah. He's on his way downstairs. Not as quick as he used to be.'

The dogs finished eating, and their attention swung back to her. They weren't in attack mode yet, but they were definitely not happy to have an intruder on their turf. She looked at her cousin's body language. He didn't seem bothered by their aggression.

'I saw you in town last night.' She walked closer to the house, slowly, her gaze on the dogs. They were pacing and watching her as if waiting to be given the order to attack.

'Did you? I was having a few drinks with friends. We'd been hunting.'

'Get much?'

'Enough. Grab a seat.' He didn't tell the dogs to lie down or sit, he was happy to have them patrol and watch her.

It was unsettling. Her uncle pushed his way out the door. He looked at the dogs and pointed. They both jumped off the porch to sit on the grass and watch from a few yards away.

'You need to keep them under control, boy.'

'I'm no boy,' Theo snarled.

'You're my boy and this is my house. Get me some coffee. You?' Her Uncle Bert tuned his gaze to her.

'Yes, that would be great.' Maybe coffee could erase the chill that was spreading through her gut. She put her phone on voice record but left it in her pocket. She was being overly paranoid, she was sure. Maybe the break-in at Gil's shop had unsettled her more than she wanted to admit.

The door swung closed and Bert shook his head. 'What did you come here for?'

'I wanted to talk to you about the River Man.'

Bert spat and shook his head again. 'I got nothing to say about him either.'

She had to get to the point with her uncle or he'd get up and go in and that would be that. 'When I was six, I saw you fighting with him.'

In the house a phone rang. Theo answered and his voice became a murmur as he spoke to whoever had called.

Bert stared at her. 'And what exactly did you see?'

She turned and pointed to where she had been hiding. 'I was there, and you were where that blue sedan is. He attacked and I closed my eyes. When I opened my eyes, you were both gone and I ran home to tell Mom you had been taken, but there you were chatting to her as if nothing had happened.'

'Maybe nothing did. Did you think of that? You were always making up stories and playing imaginary games.'

'Bert. We know the River Man is a hoax. Do you know who he is?'

Bert said nothing. 'Where's that damn boy and my coffee?'

'Bert. This person is dangerous. He needs to be stopped.'

Her uncle nodded. 'Yeah, he does.'

'So you'll tell me what you know?'

'I don't know anything.'

She stared at him.

The door opened and Theo had three cups of coffee in his hand. 'Here you go. Having a nice chat?'

Bert grunted.

Jasmine looked at her cousin. 'You came down to the interviews. Do you have a River Man story?'

Theo laughed. 'I have plenty of stories. But I'm not spilling my guts to a TV crew.'

'What about to me? It can be anonymous. We know it's a hoax, we just want to find out who's keeping the myth alive.' They knew something, she was sure. She was used to talking to people about their experiences, but Bert and Theo didn't seem scared of what they'd seen. Maybe they were staying quiet to spite her.

'Whoever it is, they are doing this town a favour. The festival is huge now.' Theo sipped his coffee.

Jasmine picked hers up to warm her hands. 'Yeah it is. Not like when I lived here.'

'You should have stayed gone. Not poked your nose in.' Bert drank the scalding hot coffee without flinching.

'I'm just doing my job.'

Theo nodded. 'And I'm doing mine.'

Bert put his hand on Theo's arm. 'Don't be a fool, boy.'

'I got orders.' Theo shook off his father's grip and stood.

Jasmine stood too. Theo was a good six inches taller. She rarely felt short, but right now she did. And she felt vulnerable. That wasn't a good feeling at all. Her heartbeat picked up and cool sweat trickled down her spine. 'What are you talking about?'

'You're going to help me make people believe in the River Man again, since you damaged his reputation.'

She laughed but it came out higher pitched and more nervous than she'd have liked. 'He isn't real.'

Were Luke and Cal already at the meeting with the mayor? It had been decided that it might be best if she wasn't there. They were saying that the footage had been dropped off anonymously. If she wasn't there, then she didn't have to lie and drop Simon in the mess.

'You and me can make him real.'

She really hoped her phone was still recording. She shook her head. 'I've got to get back to town.'

She put her foot on the first step. Theo whistled to the dogs. They sat up ready for action.

'Dare you to run,' Theo said.

She wasn't stupid. Running would only make the dogs think she was prey.

She was the prey.

'You're the River Man.' She tried to keep an eye on the dogs and her cousin. Her uncle was still sitting in his chair and drinking his coffee. 'Bert?'

'I told you he needed stopping. He's gone too far.' But he didn't get up or make a move to help her. 'Too much killing.'

'It was Theo you were fighting with that evening.' It had been Theo who'd killed that hunter and all the deer. 'Why kill?'

Theo had that wild look in his eyes that some animals got before they attacked. What did she have that she could use as a weapon? Her phone and keys. That was all. Her bag was in the car. She hadn't come here expecting trouble. She should've known better;

this was her family she was dealing with after all. If she ran, she'd never make it to the fence. She wouldn't even make it to the car.

'Why not?' He pulled something out of his pocket.

'River Man was only meant to keep prying eyes out. I told you this would happen, boy.'

'And I said shut up, Dad.'

The dogs were at the bottom of the stairs now, lips drawn back. Oh God, if he let them tear her apart ... 'Theo, I'll drive away and tell people it was a mistake.'

'Gone too far for that. I have to keep it real.' He grinned.

'Why?' If she was going to die for exposing the truth, she wanted all the answers. Maybe someone would find her phone. No. She was going to live. She was not going to get killed by a local myth—she could imagine the awful tabloid headings. *Cryptozoologist killed by cryptid hoax.*

'I got a business to protect.' He snapped a black cable tie between his hands. 'Now, put your hands behind your back.'

She frowned. What business? They were mechanics. What did mechanics have to do with the River Man? She pleaded with her uncle. 'Bert, please. Mom will be crushed. You can't let him kill me.'

Why was he just sitting there as though he didn't give a damn his son was a killer? The truth hit her hard, Bert knew. He'd always known.

'She got over your disappearance last time. She'll get over it again.' He sipped his coffee like nothing was wrong, but his face had taken on a sour expression.

'But you'll know the truth.'

'I've been keeping secrets my whole life. Think Theo is the first River Man in the family? Use your damn brain, child. You got your degree, but you can't quite work it out.' He hauled himself out of the chair. 'Don't be feeding her heart to the dogs, you got it?'

Theo curled his lip but nodded.

'Bert, please.'

He walked inside and shut the door. *Shit.*

It was just her and Theo and his dogs. If it weren't for the dogs, she would have stood a chance, but he knew he had her covered.

'Do it, Jas. Start yelling or running and let my dogs have some fun.'

\*\*\*

The glazier was suddenly fully booked and couldn't get to the shop until Tuesday at the earliest. Gil suspected that was bullshit and this was another reminder that he had stepped over the invisible line. He was no longer the good boy. What had Jasmine once said? His halo was always on and polished bright and she'd wanted to knock it off. At the time he'd thought she was joking.

That halo had granted him privileges he hadn't appreciated. Now his halo was on the ground, he was seeing the town from the other side and he wasn't liking what he saw or the way he was being treated. It was wrong.

It would be so easy to pick up that damn halo, beg forgiveness, and have the mayor or his father put it back on his head and call him respectable again. Screw that.

He didn't need their goddamn approval to live his life.

Maybe he should sell up and go somewhere else.

That idea terrified him. He couldn't imagine living somewhere where he didn't know most people, or at least their families. He liked the small-town community atmosphere.

Or he had liked it.

Now it was oppressive, like the weight of the air before a storm. His cell phone rang and he was very tempted to ignore it. He didn't want to talk to anyone besides Jasmine and she had to work all day—that had been her excuse for not staying the night. He wanted to believe her, but he suspected that she was worried about the trouble she was bringing to his door.

He closed his eyes and let the phone ring out.

It wasn't her bringing the trouble, it was everyone not minding their own business and being prissy.

The phone started up again. He didn't know the number; it wasn't

Jasmine or anyone he knew. Random person calling to warn him to behave? Maybe his phone number had been scrawled in the toilets at the petrol station on the way out of town.

He answered. 'Hello.'

'Gilbert?' A man's voice said.

No one called him Gilbert in town. He was on guard now. 'Yes.'

'It's Luke. Is Jasmine with you? We were meant to meet fifteen minutes ago to shoot some stuff.'

Until then Gil had always thought that blood draining from one's head to one's toes was a stupid saying, but he felt every drop slide away. Cold raced up his spine to fill the void left by his retreating blood. 'She left here around eleven last night. I haven't seen her since. Have you tried her phone?'

As soon as he said it, he knew how dumb that was. Of course Luke had tried her phone.

'Yeah. She's not answering. She went to see her family this morning. Do you know where they live?'

'I'll pick you up in five.'

Gil was there in four minutes. He'd closed the shop; let people think it was because of the damage. He didn't care. It was too suspicious that Jasmine had suddenly vanished. Or maybe he was being paranoid. Having his shop vandalised hadn't exactly helped his mood or his willingness to comply with what the town expected from him.

Luke got in and Gil started driving before the TV investigator had even buckled up. 'The meeting with your people went as well as could be expected. They were not impressed.'

'That's predictable.' Gil would've been shocked if they'd welcomed the news.

'The show's still going ahead. We have the footage. The police also have the footage.'

'And Jasmine wasn't in the meeting?'

'No, we decided that wouldn't be a good idea given how popular she is. Not that it mattered. Your father made the right noises about catching whoever was behind it.' Luke looked at him. 'You people didn't actually think it was real?'

Gil turned a corner and kept his eyes on the road. They passed one of the churches. 'People believe in a whole lot of things with less evidence.'

'But your father...'

Gil shook his head. 'I don't know who he is anymore. He was the one who made Jasmine leave ten years ago to break us up. I moved out of home. That rift hasn't healed.' And if anything had happened to Jasmine, it never would. His father hated her, but would he go so far as to hurt her? 'Maybe she just lost track of time?'

Luke stared at him.

Gil glanced at him. 'What?'

'Jasmine doesn't lose track of time.'

'Car broke down?' Or car got sabotaged.

'Yeah, I hope that's what it is. Car problems.' Luke didn't sound convinced at all.

Gil was quiet for a few moments; he didn't believe it either. Traffic in town was appalling. How many people were here for the festival? Had word travelled about the recent River Man kills? 'Unless the person playing River Man has decided to upgrade from deer.'

Luke's phone rang. He listened for a moment. 'Another deer was found last night.'

'Shit.'

Luke was still on the phone but giving Gil quick updates. 'Ranger has the body. Cal is going out there—with a cameraman.'

'He should take a cop.' A cameraman would only be able to film what was happening.

'Billy is ex-army, River Man wouldn't know what hit him if he tried anything.' Luke made a few more noises of agreement and hung up.

Gil pulled into the driveway of the rundown little house. 'I'll go and ask Mrs Thorpe if she's seen Jasmine.'

'The car isn't here.'

'I didn't see it on the way either.'

'I'm going to call the ranger. He was a bit too keen on the River Man.' Luke was already dialling.

Gil got out of the car and walked up the driveway. He'd never knocked on her mother's door before. He'd honk his horn from the end of the driveway and wait for Jasmine to come running out.

He drew in a breath, held it for a moment and wished he was here under better circumstances. It only took a few seconds for Mrs Thorpe to open the door. She'd have been pretty once. Fine-boned and fair-haired, a lot like Jasmine. Now she looked tired and washed-out.

'Did Jasmine stop by this morning?'

Mrs Thorpe frowned. 'No, she never called either.' She glanced past Gil. 'What's going on? Is Jasmine in trouble?'

'She didn't show up for filming. We know she was looking into a few sensitive matters.'

'About the River Man.' Her lips thinned. 'I told her to leave that alone.'

'They have proof it's a hoax.'

Her face paled and she stepped back. 'Oh Lord. Let me call my brother.'

Luke had gotten out of the car and was walking over. 'The cops have the ranger in custody. They're blaming him for the hoax and the deer kills.'

'What? He was the one who handed over the video.' This was making less and less sense.

'They're saying that he wanted to be famous.'

Gil shook his head. 'No, he only moved to Bitterwood ... six or seven years ago. There had already been deer kills before then.' The ranger wasn't the man they were after ... his father should know that the timeline wasn't right.

He did not want to be thinking that his father was well aware of that fact.

If his father knew that, then his father knew who the River Man was.

From the house came Mrs Thorpe's voice. 'I don't care, Bert, where is my Jasmine? No. That isn't a good enough reason.'

'Stop arguing with your brother. He knows best,' came a man's too loud voice. 'Damn women not thinking. Get the strangers off my porch, I don't want trouble.'

Silence. Or a very quiet conversation.

Gil looked away and stared at the car bodies over the fence, anywhere so it didn't look as though he'd been eavesdropping.

Mrs Thorpe came back to the doorway. 'You'll be wanting to go and see my brother, Bert Royle. He lives over there. Apparently it was him Jasmine saw this morning.'

Gil went down a step. The wood sagged under his boot.

'Watch out for his dogs, Theo trains them up to be mean.' She glanced back into the house then lowered her voice. 'Please find her before it's too late.'

'Is there anything else you can tell us?' Luke smiled. He was all charm when he needed to be.

She shook her head.

Gil tugged at Luke's arm. He didn't want to be making trouble for Jasmine's mother, and it was clear she was already in some bother with her husband. 'Let's take the car in case of the dogs.'

The gate to Bert's property was open and there were no dogs racing out to meet them. The whole place had a deserted air about it. There were cars everywhere, and anyone could be hiding in the metal jungle.

Gil scanned the yard. 'Do you see the rental?'

'No. Could be round the back?'

'I'm not doing a lap around the back. I'll go knock on the door.' This was a friendly visit to a man who'd seen Jasmine this morning. He didn't dare call it into the cops. He didn't trust anyone right now.

'And get eaten by the dogs.'

'Thanks.' Gil didn't mind dogs, but ones that were bred up to be guard dogs, well that was a different matter. All the rumours about Bert Royle resurfaced. Sure he was a mechanic, but his place was occasionally searched by the cops. Too many cars went through there, he remembered his father saying. He waited a moment before he got out of the car. Still no sign of the dogs. 'The ranger had cameras up, right? Do we know where they are?'

'No. He didn't say.'

'Would you know how to hack into them?'

Luke raised an eyebrow. 'My job is to stand around and talk about old myths and new urban legends.'

'What about Calvin?'

'Cal ... might be able to get an exclusive with the man who took the footage. If the ranger is smart, he'll play along now instead of being anonymous.'

'The police will be listening. They'll learn where the cameras are too.' Gil didn't know if that was a good or bad thing. He should be able to trust the cops, and his father. He didn't. If anything, he was laying part of the blame at his father's feet for doing so little over the years.

'Got a better idea?'

Gil had nothing. Chatting to Bert wasn't high on his list either. 'You talk to your people and I'll go and get eaten by dogs.'

'I like that plan.' Luke grinned, then put his hand on Gil's arm. 'Be careful, I need you alive. You know this town and the people. They won't talk to me.'

They weren't talking to him either.

# Chapter 11

The cable tie cut into Jasmine's wrists. The boot was dark, and the air was stuffy. Whatever the last user of the rental car had put in here had left a sour tang that was lodged at the back of her throat. The vehicle swung around the corner, and her shoulder slammed into the edge. She hissed but refused to cry out. The dogs barked on the back seat, excited as if they knew what was to come.

She was not going to panic. Or at least she wasn't going to give into the panic that was flooding her body.

If it weren't for the dogs, she wouldn't be in the boot of her car. She'd have kicked down the seats and fought her cousin to the end. She twisted a little more, so her head pressed against the back of the seats. She really hoped it was as easy to kick out a taillight as it looked in the movies.

When Theo stopped the car, it was all over. She knew that. She'd heard the stats about what happened when the killer arrived at their destination.

No amount of pleading had stopped Theo from doing what he thought he had to do.

*They were blood.*

*Think of her mother.*

But he didn't care. She'd vanished once; this time it would be permanent. This time people would look for her. She gave the light another kick, and again. That time it came free. If they were already too far out of town, no one would notice the missing taillight anyway.

Theo had her phone, so that wasn't going to help her. She needed to get her hands around the front before the car stopped. She couldn't get caught halfway.

She started squirming, sweat slicking her skin and adrenaline making her heart race. She was not dying in Bitterwood.

The River Man, Theo, would not get another victim.

She was too goddamn chewy.

That was what Tricia had called her when she'd first moved in. The resentment and fear had become a shield to keep people away. As a result, friends were hard to make because there was just too much gristle to work through before they got to the real Jasmine.

She gritted her teeth and grunted as the cable tie dug deeper into her wrists, tearing her skin, but then her hands were in front of her, not behind her. She panted. The warm air sticking in her lungs and making it hard to breathe. She closed her eyes and tried to be calmer. She needed to be thinking clearly if she was going to survive.

Gil had always been able to cut through her walls and find her.

*Please be looking for me, Gil.*

\*\*\*

Gil walked up the steps, ready to reach up and grab the edge of the porch roof if the dogs suddenly appeared, but the house was quiet. Too quiet. If Jasmine had been here and spoken to someone, they were now gone. His heart sank.

He knocked, not expecting an answer.

Footsteps plodded through the house.

Gil stepped back and glanced around looking for something he could use as a weapon but saw nothing. There was no scuffle of dog feet or barking.

Bert opened the door. He had nice pants and a button-up shirt on, like he was going somewhere. In his hand was one of his hunting rifles.

Gil took another step back. 'I didn't come here looking for trouble. I just want to know where Jasmine is.'

'You already know where to find her. Quit wasting time here.'

She was with the River Man, or whoever was playing the River Man. They already suspected that. But the River Man's territory stretched for miles along the river. He hoped Calvin was having some luck with getting that interview with the ranger, who must be regretting ever helping Jasmine. 'Who has her?'

'Can't say.' Bert pressed his lips together.

'She's your niece.' How could Bert just stand there when he knew what was going to happen?

'And he's my son.' His face crumpled, but he pulled himself back together. 'I thought handing the job onto him would help him, but it made him worse. Gave him an excuse.'

Gil stared at Bert. His son. He didn't know Theo well, he was about ten years older, but there'd been stories and everyone knew how much he liked to hunt. 'Why is Theo the River Man?'

Bert shook his head. 'I tried to stop him.'

'Where's he taken Jasmine.'

'Be a better man than your father.' Bert lifted the rifle. 'Than me.'

Gil drew in a breath, but the bullet wasn't for him. Bert put the muzzle under his chin and pulled the trigger. Blood splashed on Gil's face. He stood there, not sure what had happened for a moment. As the echo of the shot faded away and Bert fell to the ground, it all became real. This wasn't a harmless hoax, a way of getting money into the town. People were dying and willing to die to protect what was going on.

'Bert!' Gil dropped to his knees. But Bert was well and truly dead.

A car door slammed and Luke raced toward him.

Luke cursed. 'He's dead.' Luke swore again. 'I have to call the cops and the ambulance.'

Gil was still kneeling on the old porch. The old man had dressed to die. He didn't get this dressed up for church—when he went. Gil wasn't sure that he'd ever seen Bert in nice pants and shirt. The old man knew people would want to talk to him, and he wasn't going to rat on his son.

Family loyalty, no matter what.

That wasn't always a good thing.

Gil stood. He needed to go. 'I have to find Jasmine.'

He shouldn't be leaving the scene. He'd be questioned by the cops. And while all of that happened, Theo would be killing Jasmine and getting away with it because the only man who knew the truth was dead.

*Be a better man than your father.*

No ... his father knew the truth.

Luke hung up. 'If you're going to save Jasmine, you'd best do it now before everyone arrives.'

Gil nodded. 'His son is the River Man ... I don't know why. But he also referenced my father.'

'Right. I'll keep my mouth closed about being clued in.'

'Might be safest.' What the hell was going on? He thought he'd known this place and everyone in it. Maybe he only knew what he was told. That would be the same for most folk.

'Get going, or they might pass you and stop you.' Luke gave him a push.

Gil nodded. His gaze kept drifting back to Bert. When he closed his eyes, he could feel the blood hit his skin. He wiped his face with his sleeve.

Luke grabbed his arm and propelled him in the direction of the stairs. 'There's nothing you can do for him. You know where the River Man likes to leave the bodies. Go and save Jasmine before it's too late.'

He knew he had to go. Luke would get lost and the farmers wouldn't want a stranger on their property.

'They'll ask how you got here.'

'And I'll say we were together, but you took off to find her before it was too late. I'll tell them that truth.'

Gil gave a single nod, then ran to the car. Someone would have to tell Mrs Thorpe that her brother was dead.

He didn't want to be telling her that her daughter was dead.

*** 

The car slowed down and after a few minutes came to a stop. The sick sense of dread rose up, swamping Jasmine and making it hard to breathe. She was going to have to fight. All she'd found in the back of the car was a pen. Why did hire cars not have tool kits or first-aid kits or anything useful?

She hoped someone had seen the kicked-out taillight and called it in, but she wasn't going to hold her breath for help. She was on her own and she had to get herself out of this. Why couldn't this have been a nice cryptid with a cheesy festival story? Why did it have to be hoax with a killer behind the mask?

Her cousin.

The dogs got out of the car and started yipping, keyed up with the promise of a hunt and blood. Her blood.

She'd never been one for praying, and she didn't have time to start now, but she hoped that someone was on her side and that she'd not wind up dead with her heart fed to the dogs.

Even if she fought off her cousin, there were still the dogs.

She'd have to get in the car and drive away.

Theo had a gun; she wouldn't get far unless she got that off him.

There were so many things to consider. So many ways for this to go wrong. More wrong.

He was talking to the dogs, telling them to calm down. He knocked on the boot of the car. 'Still alive in there, Jas?'

She didn't answer. Let him wonder.

'Don't be like that. You brought this on yourself for being a nosy bitch. If you'd minded your own business and looked out for your family, none of this would have happened. But no, you took off to the city and cut us all off.' He banged on the boot again. 'Talk to me or I might have to make a few air holes with bullets.'

Fear struck her heart. If he shot her, she was screwed.

'I don't understand why you are doing this, being the River Man,' she clarified. She knew why he was killing her, for being a nosy bitch. He'd made that clear. And her uncle had done nothing.

'I'm protecting my family. The same way Dad did and his dad before.'

The River Man had always been in her family. It hadn't been a fight she'd seen but her uncle helping Theo out of costume. Was he dressed up now? Was anyone watching the ranger's cameras? She didn't even know if they were in view of a camera. She hoped Simon was paying attention and that Theo was stupid enough to go back to one of his favourite dumping grounds. Someone would find her.

Hopefully while she was still breathing.

'What are you protecting your family from?'

He laughed. The dogs were carrying on, barking and playing. The boot popped open and sunlight streamed in. She squinted at the sudden brightness.

'From people like you. People who stick their noses in where it doesn't concern them.' Her cousin stared down at her. 'You owe us. Your mother owes us, and yet you want to bring it all down.'

'I just wanted to learn about the River Man.' That hadn't changed. 'I never thought he was real.'

He pulled on a glove that glinted in the sun; the fingertips had claws. Sharp claws. The fear that had been under control broke free and pinched her heart. 'Bullshit, Jas. You were smart enough to learn the truth, but not smart enough to shut up? What did you want? The glory of uncovering the truth? Of shutting down the family business?'

'What family business?'

Theo stared at her. There was no compassion in his eyes. This was a man who regularly killed and mutilated deer and who'd killed at least one man. He reached in with the clawed glove to pull her out. She shrank back and lashed out with her feet. He snagged the leg of her jeans, and her calf, cutting her and dragging her out. She cried out.

He released her leg and grabbed her arm, the tips of his claws digging into her flesh. 'A little of this and a little of that.' He hauled her up so she was standing in front of him. The dogs circled her legs, sniffing her blood. 'The River Man has kept our family safe for generations. Stopped the nosy folk from prying when we rustled horses. And has kept prying eyes from the car rustling.'

'Car rustling?' She couldn't help the tremble in her knees. She'd rather fight Theo than his dogs. Maybe she could keep him talking.

'We strip 'em and send them over the border,' he said with pride. 'Sometimes we send a little something else too. Something the chief don't know about.'

Jasmine stared at him. The dogs snarled and circled, getting closer and closer, she wanted to climb back into the boot. 'What does he have to do with it?'

'All book smarts and no common sense ... money, Jas. It's always about money.'

'You bribe him?'

'I prefer to think of it as an operating license fee.'

Gil's father had known all along who the River Man was. Worse, the chief had been protecting Theo all these years because he was making some easy money off her family's crimes. No wonder he hadn't wanted Gil getting close to her, the truth might have come out and ruined everything. But it was over anyway—Theo had killed too many deer and attracted too much attention. And if she died, Luke and Cal wouldn't let it go unsolved. 'Did you kill that man twenty years ago?'

Theo smiled. 'My first. I took his heart to put my touch on the River Man.'

'Why kill him at all?' She needed to know why, even if it was to take to her grave.

One of the dogs licked the blood from her leg. She flinched, it took every ounce of will not to leap away or lash out.

'He likes you. Likes the taste of you. Dad said I couldn't feed your heart to them, but he won't know, will he? Not until it's too late.'

The cuts were stinging. The dogs wouldn't leave her alone now they smelled her blood. Would they get too interested and bite? How well did Theo have them trained?

'Did Bert make you do this?' How old had Theo been when Bert had told him the truth about the River Man and brought him in on the secret?

Theo smiled and flexed his clawed glove. Dark green and with curved secateurs blades for the claws, it looked well-constructed, and it certainly caused damage. Worse if she ran and he grabbed hard, he could tear muscle or rip open an artery.

Before she ran, she needed to know where she was running to.

Without it being obvious, she snuck a glance to her left and away from Theo. She shifted her weight and tested out her injured leg. It hurt, but nothing felt ruined. She still had to get rid of the dogs so they wouldn't give chase.

Theo got the dogs to sit. They watched her, anticipating what was to come.

'Dad has nothing to do with this. He didn't have the guts to do what needed to be done. He left the occasional deer kill to be blamed on the River Man, but he didn't put thought into it. People needed to be afraid. The chief needed to be reminded that he couldn't order us around.' Theo had the same gleam of expectation as the dogs.

She didn't know if she should admit she was afraid or deny it. Her cousin clearly enjoyed his role. 'So you killed the deer more regularly to keep the fear fresh.' But he'd gone too far and modern technology meant the deaths could be examined.

'You're smart. Always thought yourself too good for here.' He grabbed her arm and pulled her around the car. She cried out, hoping that maybe they were close enough that someone would hear her. He backhanded her with his ungloved hand. 'Shut your mouth.'

The dogs were racing around again, waiting and whining. Were they waiting for her to run?

He led her away from the car and the river. 'I thought you killed closer to the river ... that would make sense for an amphibious creature. He'd grab deer that stopped for a drink.'

Theo took another step and looked at her. 'Did you analyse what I'd done? Is that what gave it away?'

She swallowed and ignored the burning of her arm where his claws were digging in. She wouldn't struggle yet. If she could get him to take her to the river, she could make her escape. Or drown in the process, given that her hands were tied, but she was willing to take that chance.

'Of course I studied the evidence. That's my job; to work out if it's a real animal or a cryptid or a hoax. Some of the River Man's behaviour didn't add up.' Some of what she was saying was lies. But right now she'd say anything if it gave her a few seconds to run.

The dogs barked at the delay and Theo hushed them. They obeyed him. That was good, and bad if he told them to hunt her down. Right now she had his interest. 'Oh yes, there are all kinds of clues that a zoologist would look for. Little tells.'

Did he know about the video?

He watched her with cold eyes. She expected him to slap her again for knowing too much. Her mouth tasted like blood and her sock was wet with blood from the cuts on her leg. They'd probably need stitching.

His claws tightened and she yelped. Her cousin smiled. This wasn't just about protecting the family, this was fun. He enjoyed killing.

'You could have so much fun with the River Man, really get people going. Footprints in the mud. Fake eggs, like those mermaids' purses that are actually shark eggs. The River Man would need a mate. Even turtles don't live forever, they need to breed.'

'You offering to help?' She didn't like the curl of his lip. 'I don't think you are. You mucking around with the Easton boy has put everything at risk. Bit of a pattern for you, isn't it? Just like Tricia. Must be your father's blood because Royles look after family, they don't leave it.'

'The chief forced me to leave or he'd go after my family.' Which made more sense now she knew that he was protecting her family and taking bribes. He must have thought she knew what her uncle was up to and would spill the secret. In reality she'd known nothing;

she'd only wanted to stop the cops from harassing her family. That was never going to stop when the Eastons and Royles were in bed together. 'I left to protect you.'

If she hadn't, would the chief have made good on his threat or would he have found himself caught between easy money and doing what was right? This could've ended ten years ago if she'd been brave enough to stand up to a bully.

'When did he start taking payment to look the other way?' Or had it always been that way between the families. One family ran the hoax and took the risk while the other was the law and looked away as long as they were receiving bribes.

Theo yanked her toward the river. 'You're going to take a swim. Guess you must have fallen in while checking out the River Man's hunting grounds and he took you. Dangerous to be out here alone, Jas. You should know better.' He gave her a shove that sent her sprawling to the ground in front of the car.

Were the keys in the ignition?

Could she get in and drive away?

The dogs were around her immediately, barking in her face. She struggled up, her hands still bound. Theo opened the car door. Was he going to leave her here with the dogs? No, he was getting his gun.

She inched around as if trying to get away from the dogs, when all she wanted to see was if the keys were in the car so she could drive away.

Her cousin grinned at her and then produced the key from his shirt pocket. 'I might not have a degree, but I'm not dumb, Jas. I've been doing this a while. They just don't find them all.'

Her blood chilled. There'd been other human victims of the River Man, Theo, she corrected, or was he talking about deer?

'Do you hide them deliberately?'

'Too many human deaths will make everyone too worried. I've watched those TV shows where the cops hunt down serial killers. I'm not like them. I'm the River Man. This has been going for generations and will keep going.'

River Men in the past hadn't killed as often, they'd relied on the myth and the occasional sighting for their power. Theo wanted to be more than a story and that would be his undoing. He'd already made people like the ranger look hard into what was happening. People were smarter and better educated than they had been even twenty years ago, and these days they had access to better technology, like cameras that could be set up to monitor wildlife, and smartphones. People wanted to investigate the myths and urban legends and see what was beneath.

Usually there was nothing.

She wished there'd been nothing.

If the chief was mixed up in this, it would not end well and Gil would get caught in the spatter. There was nothing she could do to protect him. She couldn't even protect herself.

Theo slammed the door. 'To the river, so you can die properly.'

'With a bullet?'

'One through the heart, it will hardly hurt. Once the dogs are done with you, no one will be any the wiser.'

Gil would know. Her crew would know. The secret was already out. Theo just didn't want to believe it.

'It's going to be awful finding the body of my cousin after a morning of hunting.' He fired the rifle into the trees to prove the point. 'Pity I didn't catch anything.'

She walked backwards to the river, not willing to take her eyes off him. Would he shoot her once she was in?

He didn't seem too bothered. He followed with slow easy steps, the dogs at his heels, glove on one hand, rifle in the other. She glanced over her shoulder. The river was only a few steps away. She needed to make a decision. Tackle Theo, or jump in and hope that the current would get her away before he shot her and that she didn't drown.

Jasmine flexed her wrists, but there was no give in the cable tie. There was really only one option.

# Chapter 12

Gil drove out of town; he wasn't going to risk getting caught in traffic or stopped by his father. Once out, he drove a little too fast toward the bridge so he could cross the river and head toward the farms that backed onto the river, the River Man's usual hunting territory.

He slowed at the intersection. Would Theo have driven on one of the tracks that ran alongside the farms and risked being seen? If he was smart, he wouldn't be going back to where the deer was most recently found. It was too obvious.

The indicator ticked. Gil didn't know where he was going. The stretch of river known to be used by the creature, man, was too vast. But Theo hadn't always been the River Man. He turned away from the farms and hoped he was making the right decision.

His phone buzzed. *Cops have arrived.*

They would now be looking for him and his role in the death of Bert Royle.

He hadn't been involved, but if his father was looking to cover his ass then Gil was sure he'd be stitched up just like everyone else. Poor man hounded to death by TV show, or something like that. He hoped the TV show had good lawyers.

The first deer had been found up this way. If there was no sign of Jasmine or Theo, he'd start walking down river.

His phone rung. 'Hello?'

No answer. There was some talking in the background.

He did not need some random butt-dial. He was about to hang up when someone spoke up. 'Chief, I'd appreciate talking to the ranger.'

Calvin was talking to his father and letting him listen in.

'No, absolutely not. The man is responsible for several deer deaths.'

'As are plenty of people who hunt.' Calvin's voice was dry. 'I was under the impression that the deer deaths started before he arrived. Also the man in the footage doesn't look at all like the ranger. The hair colour is wrong for a start.'

There was silence for a moment. 'Don't you think you people have caused enough trouble? Sweeping in and poking around.'

'Uncovering the truth about your River Man? You have a killer in your town, Chief. Does that concern you?'

'That unsolved murder from twenty years ago? You're worried about that?'

'I'm worried that your River Man has my zoologist. I know you ran her out of town once before.'

'Think very carefully about your next words, Calvin LeRoux.'

Gil held his breath. Goading his father had never been a smart move. 'I just want to know if you had people out looking for her, monitoring the ranger's cameras.'

'How many cops do you think this town has? Bert Royle just killed himself. Your zoologist has probably taken herself off to investigate and poke her nose into other peoples' business.'

'She's not answering her phone. I'm worried. Perhaps you could lend me the ranger ... oh that's right. You arrested him for deer mutilation, even though they started before he arrived.'

'Get out of my office,' his father thundered.

Footsteps and a door shutting. After a moment Calvin spoke directly into the phone as his voice was clear and loud. 'I tried. Tell me you have something?'

Gil drew in a breath. 'Nothing. I've headed north. Can you get to the ranger's office? If the cops are too busy...'

'On it. Where is it?'

Nowhere near where he was. Gil had always thought Bitterwood was a small town, right now it seemed huge and his odds of finding Jasmine alive were tiny.

\*\*\*

The river would be cold, and she had no idea how deep it was. If she stumbled back she could land on her ass with her head above water, or she could go under and be swallowed up. She was trying to work out exactly where she was. North or south of town? She couldn't see or hear any sounds that would indicate civilisation was close.

Theo had confidently fired the rifle into the trees, which meant he didn't expect company.

Her heart hammered. Her chest ached, but the adrenaline was keeping her alive. She had to be grateful she was still alive. She looked at her cousin. He was ten years older, and while they'd never been close, they'd never had arguments either. She'd always been the little girl who was hanging around with the boys—not that she'd had much choice. Her only playmates had been her cousins. Even after she'd started school, there'd still been a distance between her and the other kids. One she suspected the Royles of cultivating.

Theo lifted the rifle. 'Nice clean shot, you don't want to move and have me shoot you multip—'

She didn't hear the rest of the words. The water closed over her head. She kicked away, needing to put distance between Theo and his rifle, knowing that she had to keep her head below. The moment she popped up, he'd take a shot.

The noise of his rifle reached her even through the water. But no bullet hit her. The glove must be affecting his accuracy. And she was a moving target, partially hidden by the water.

Her lungs burned.

*Not yet.*

Black dots danced behind her eyelids.

*Not yet.*

Would she be able to surface? How deep was she? Her hands were still tied and she couldn't use them very well. Fear made her kick up and she risked a breath. She sucked in water that splashed in her face and coughed, struggling to keep her head above water.

Theo was shouting to the dogs.

*Shit.*

She hadn't gone far. The dogs were racing along the riverbank, crashing through the undergrowth. Her eyes widened as one looked at her. It started barking and she dove back under and started kicking hard, willing the current to sweep her far enough that she could find somewhere to crawl out and hide.

It would have to be on the other side of the river as the dogs had her scent. Theo would keep searching. She'd have to get far away. Far enough that

Theo would hopefully think she'd drowned. If she stopped too soon, she was dead.

The cold of the river was already in her bones. If she stayed too long in the river, she was dead.

***

Gil had parked the car and was on foot. He couldn't travel the riverbanks in a car. He was hoping that Calvin would call him back with news from the ranger's cameras, but he wasn't holding his breath.

He was so tempted to start calling out, but that wouldn't help.

What he needed to do was get other people looking. People who wouldn't mind lending a hand if he let them believe that the police were shorthanded because of the festival. He called up a few friends and asked if they could keep a look out for the hire car and Jasmine. He also asked that if they saw Theo to get him to contact the chief about a serious family matter.

Word would've already gotten around about Bert's death.

Tyler offered to grab his father's runabout. A tiny boat that had been at the centre of their summer fun when they'd finished high school. Gil wasn't sure the thing was still safe to sit in, but right now it didn't matter if he had to bail it out as he went.

Gil rang his father to tell him that Theo had taken Jasmine. Time was sliding away to find her alive.

'They're related. Of course they'll go places together.' His father sounded as if he couldn't give a damn.

'Dad, he took her because she knows too much about the River Man.' Things his father knew. 'Bert confessed before he shot himself. Theo is responsible for the unsolved murder and the deer mutilations.'

'If you were there, you need to come in. You shouldn't have left the scene.'

'I'm looking for Jasmine before she's the River Man's next victim. I suggest you do the same, Dad. Bert told me everything.' He was lying through his teeth and making wild stabs in pitch-black, but as the silence grew he knew he'd scored a hit.

'It's your word, and that of a dead man, against mine. I'm the chief, I have the respect of the people.' His father's voice was as hard and as slippery as ice.

'The word of an Easton against a Royle. That's how it worked, wasn't it. Both families used to rustle horses, but somehow the Eastons managed to come out looking good while the Royles kept the hoax going.'

'You shut your mouth and stay away from that family.' Anger reverberated through his father's voice.

'You'd better pray I find Jasmine alive.' Gil hung up. His hand shaking.

Tyler came around the corner in the runabout that had truly seen better days. The engine idled with a definite lumpiness. Gil waded into the water and climbed in. 'Seen anything?'

'Nothing between Dad's place and here.' He shook his head. 'If she's in the water...'

If she was in the water she'd be heading downstream, and if she was in the water there was a good chance they'd be pulling out a corpse.

Last night she'd been warm in his arms. They'd talked about anything but what was going to happen when she left. He didn't want that to be the last time he saw her alive.

He didn't want her leaving his life for a second time.

\*\*\*

The river was leaching the heat and life from her. She didn't know how far she'd got; only that trying to keep her head down for as long as possible each time was bringing her close to drowning. Drown or get shot. Now she could add hypothermia to the list of ways to die.

She needed to get out of the water soon and she needed to get warm.

And she had no idea where she was or who she could trust beyond Gil and her crew.

When she got past the town, she'd crawl out. Find a way to free her hands and a place to hide. Would Theo give up or come after her, hunting her down until he was sure she was dead?

With her lungs burning, she exhaled and then let herself rise so she could suck in some fresh air. She glanced around, looking for landmarks or signs of life. Anything.

Nothing.

But she couldn't hear the dogs either. She kicked, slowly turning so her feet were pointing downstream so she could see where she was going. Bitterwood was coming into view.

Her jaw clenched with the cold. Her body was shaking. Not good signs, plus she was losing blood—not that she could feel the cuts as her legs were numb.

Sounds of cars and the noise of the bands playing the festival reached her. It would be easy to haul herself out of the river near the bridge. And if she were Theo, or if he had helpers, that would be exactly where she'd wait. Her cousin wasn't stupid, nor was he acting alone.

A little longer in the river. She could do it. She was going to have to go under again.

The bridge was drawing closer. Soon she'd be able to make out the people on the bridge. If she could see them, they could see her.

She drew in a few breaths, trying to get as much oxygen as she could into her lungs.

Then she went under.

***

Tyler steered the boat while Gil searched both sides of the shore. His phone rung and he didn't dare ignore it.

'I have a man and two dogs with a gun on one of the cameras,' Calvin said without an introduction.

'What does he look like?'

'Dark hair, tallish. He looked angry.'

'No sign of Jasmine?'

'None. Luke isn't answering his phone either.'

'He's probably being held regarding Bert's suicide.' Every time he blinked he saw snapshots of Bert's death. He heard the shot and felt the blood on his face.

Tyler nudged him and pointed.

Gil's gut knotted at the sight. 'I've found the hire car.'

'I don't think I'm going to get anything else from here.'

'Find somewhere to hole up. If my dad catches you, he'll find a reason to hold you if only to stop you searching.'

Calvin swore. 'I'll be in touch.'

Tyler nudged the boat in as close as he could. 'This is not right.'

Gil jumped out and climbed up the bank. He stained to hear anything over the sound of the river and the birds in the trees. Even the rustling of leaves was too loud. If Jasmine was here, he was too late. For the first time this morning, he didn't want to find her.

There were blood drops on the hood. A smear on the boot of the car and a kicked-out taillight, but no sign of Jasmine. He breathed without the crushing sensation of fear cracking his ribs. Theo was out there hunting her, according to Calvin.

That meant she was alive.

Or at least she had been the last time Theo had seen her.

'Nothing.' He made his way back to the boat. Where would she have gone?

Tyler looked at him. 'We keep heading downstream?'

'Yeah.' A twig spun past, carried on the current. 'Let's get past the town.'

They could overtake the current and catch whatever it brought them. He doubted Jasmine would ever trust anyone in Bitterwood again. Right now that didn't matter, he didn't know how badly she was hurt, or if she was even conscious.

Tyler revved the engine and they sped down the river. Gil was still looking, but this time he was watching the water, not the riverbank. Jasmine wouldn't be running, that would make it easy for her cousin to catch her. She'd be making him work.

What kind of man hunted his cousin like she was an animal? The same kind that killed and made it look like a monster was at work.

Some monsters were human, and there was nothing more to it.

He looked up at the sound of barking dogs. Theo stood on the riverbank, rifle up as though aiming at them. Gil froze, they went past him in seconds, no shot fired, but now Theo knew others were looking for Jasmine.

They were running out of time.

\*\*\*

Jasmine tried to get close to the bank, but it was harder than she'd thought it would be. If her hands had been free, and if she hadn't been so cold and tired ... Her feet touched the bottom of the river and she stumbled, going under again, before dragging herself out with her elbows. She lay on the muddy bank, shaking and coughing. Not exactly silent or hidden.

She was past the town, but not safe, not yet.

An engine, a boat, getting louder made her move, but not as fast as she'd have liked.

She had not got this far to be re-caught, or killed.

She struggled back, hoping to get into the scrub. She needed to find something to get her hands free. The little runabout came into view and she froze. If she didn't move, maybe it would go past her. Maybe it had nothing to do with her. It wasn't like she was the centre of the universe. Hardly anyone would know she was missing and fewer would care.

Part of her wanted to call out for help. She was so cold and so tired. She doubted she'd make it through the rest of the day, and certainly not the night.

The boat slowed. The people in it had seen her.

*Shit.*

'Jasmine!'

Her name from his lips was a jolt to her weary and wounded body. A shot of adrenaline that would keep her going. Was she imagining it?

No. The boat was getting closer. And it was Gil in the boat.

'Gil?' Her voice was a pathetic broken thing that barely crept past her lips.

She was going to be safe. It was going to be okay.

The boat stopped and Gil waded over to her. He put his arms around her and pulled her close. He was so warm. She wasn't listening to what he was saying. She didn't care. All she knew was that whatever happened next, she wasn't alone.

# Chapter 13

Gil took off his coat and wrapped it around Jasmine's shoulders. Her lips were blue, and her hands were like ice. He used his pocketknife to cut through the cable tie, then rubbed her hands between his. She was crying. He'd never seen her cry. That scared him. She must be really hurt.

'It's going to be okay.' He didn't see how it was ever going to be okay.

'Theo is the River Man.' She forced the words out through clamped teeth. She was shaking so bad.

'I know. My father is involved too.' He couldn't look her in the eye as he said that. All this time his father had been trying to tell him how to live his life, warning him about stepping on to the wrong side of town and there he was, taking bribes and looking the other way. 'You need to get to the hospital.'

She shook her head. 'Don't leave me.'

'I won't.' He wasn't letting her out of his sight. 'We need to go back into town.' He picked her up and carried her back to the boat.

Tyler's face was hard. For a moment Gil wasn't sure he could trust his friend. What if he'd been in on it too?

'You got a problem?'

Tyler shook his head. 'Getting caught up in a feud between the Royles and the Thorpes isn't going to end well.'

'It's bigger than that.' Gil helped Jasmine put on his coat properly and do up the buttons. He didn't tell Tyler the rest. That wasn't his to tell.

Tyler took off his cap and put it on Jasmine's head. 'Stay down. Your cousin is searching for you.' He looked at Gil. 'Where do you want to go? Your car, Dad's place or town? I'm thinking town. She doesn't look so good.' He pointed at Jasmine's leg.

Gil hadn't noticed it before, but the leg of her jeans was torn, and she was bleeding. 'Jasmine, how bad are you hurt?' Her eyes were dazed, and it took her too long to respond. 'To town. I'll carry her if I have to.'

'I'll get Angie to pick us up.'

Gil was about to make a comment about Angie not lifting a finger to help

Jasmine in the past, but he kept his mouth shut. He didn't care who helped or what their motives were. Angie would love being first on the scene for this lot of gossip.

Tyler stopped the boat just past the bridge and the picnic table. There was a small jetty that he tied the boat to. Gil climbed up, and between him and Tyler they got Jasmine up.

Angie ran down the pier in her heels; she'd obviously been at work. 'Oh my God! What happened?'

'River Man got her.' That was the truth.

Angie took a step back. 'Don't bullshit to me, Gilbert Easton. I was talking to Nancy and she said there is no River Man, it's all a big hoax. That's what the TV show people said.'

'The person pretending to be the River Man got her.' Tyler hauled himself up onto the pier. 'Not that it matters what happened, only that she needs to get to hospital.'

She was still cold to touch. 'Come on, Jas, hold on just a little longer. We'll get you warmed up and you'll feel as good as new.'

He picked her up and she curled against him. He didn't want to let her go. 'Where's your car?'

Angie looked at him. 'You really do love her.'

Did he? After all this time ... when he knew that what they had was going to end ... that they could never be together.

'Yeah.' He did love her, maybe he always had, but that didn't mean she would ever be his.

His eyes stung and he glanced down at Jasmine. She always reached deep into his life and pulled apart who he thought he was. With her he was better. He followed Angie to her car, Tyler trailing.

Music was playing in the centre. There would be stalls of cakes and crafts. Everything that made the River Man Festival so popular. It was all a lie. A lie to cover up criminal activity and then a lie to hide a man's desire to kill.

Angie stopped and Gil ran into the back of her. He looked up.

Theo was sitting on the picnic table, gun by his side. 'When I saw you, I knew you'd bring her to me.'

Gil became stone.

'I didn't do anything. I was just meeting my fiancé.' Angie put her hands up and started walking away.

Theo pointed at Gil. 'You. Mr Reliable. You don't want to risk your father's reputation, the good Easton name?'

Behind his back, Tyler was making a phone call; he was asking for the police. No ... anyone but the cops. But Tyler didn't know it all, he still trusted the police. Gil had too, now he couldn't even trust his own father.

'It's over, Theo. The truth is out. Your father is dead.' Angie's car was fifty yards away in the car park—which was a glorified gravel square with a few wooden bollards across the front to stop people from driving into the river. She was halfway to her car.

Theo jerked as though struck. 'What did you do to him?'

'He killed himself so he wouldn't be forced to turn you in.' Gil shifted Jasmine's weight. The arm that had been around his neck slid free. She was unconscious, a dead weight in his arms. The only sign of life was the lifting of her chest with each breath. She was still alive.

A cop car pulled up and Chief Easton got out.

They were drawing onlookers now. Curious locals and out-of-towners were wondering why that TV show host was looking dead and the cops were on the scene.

Angie had her car door open and was waiting for him. Gil held his father's gaze.

'Put her in my car and I'll get her to hospital.' His father's voice was level, but the challenge was there, daring him to make a scene.

Gil dared.

'I'm taking her. You should be arresting Theo.' Gil started forward.

'For what? Assisting with the search?' He was making a joke out of it, trying to bury the truth once again. His father would bury Jasmine if he could.

'I know everything, Dad. Everything. Jasmine and her team, they know too.

It's too late.' He marched toward Angie's car.

'You are wanted for questioning regarding the death of Bert Royle. You get in my car with her and wait at the station.'

'I'm taking her to hospital. You do what you need to.' He put Jasmine on the back seat and slid in next to her.

Angie started the engine. 'He's going to lock us all up.'

'Not if he has any sense, he won't.' Gil watched his father as Angie reversed the car. He was striding over to Tyler and Theo. Theo looked smug and confident. Tyler was frowning.

God, he hoped Tyler would be okay.

'What do you know, Gil? What's going on? Whenever she's around you act weird.'

No, whenever Jasmine was around he knew who he was, and he stopped being who the town expected him to be.

'It's not about her, Angie. It never was.'

His father had wanted to make sure that they hadn't gotten close because then they would have gotten close to the truth. Gil rubbed her cold hands between his. Her wet clothing had seeped into his coat. His jeans and shoes were wet and cold and clinging to his legs. How long had she been in the river for, cut and bleeding?

What had Theo cut her with?

Gil doubted that his father would arrest Theo. Somehow it would all be swept away. A lie would be told and repeated until the whole town believed that Chief Easton was the good guy and could do no wrong.

He closed his eyes.

No. That wasn't going to happen again.

\*\*\*

There was a police car waiting at the hospital for him. Gil made sure that Jasmine was seen in emergency and he gave the staff the contact detail for Luke and Calvin. The nurse who wrote this all down on Jasmine's clipboard was the daughter-in-law of one of Nancy sons. She'd been a few years ahead of him at school and from the look on her face was more than a little horrified that the chief's son was being escorted by a cop. No doubt she thought he had something to do with Jasmine's injuries.

'Will she be okay?' Gil pressed.

'I can't make any promises. Her core temperature is low. But the doctors know what to do. She isn't the first city dweller to run into trouble up here and get hypothermia.' The nurse smiled, but her eyes were on the cop shadowing Gil.

The young man wasn't going to rush Gil out, but he wasn't going to risk letting Gil slip away either.

'And the cuts?'

'They don't look too bad. She'll need some stitches once she is stabilised. There's nothing you can do, so why don't you deal with your other issue.' She indicated to the cop.

She was right, Gil knew that. But he didn't want to leave. What if someone here was in on the scam or whatever his father was running? What if she vanished again? He turned to the cop. 'Can you call her mother and let her know that we found her?'

The cop opened his mouth, and Gil was sure he was going to say no, but there was no good reason to say no, so the cop pulled out his cell phone and called Mrs Thorpe. While Mrs Thorpe knew more about the River Man than she'd let on, Gil had been there for her frantic call to her brother. She'd been worried about Jasmine.

'She's on her way.' The cop said with a nod. 'And we should be heading down to the station. The chief will be wondering where you are.'

As far as Gil was concerned, his father could wait. He had nothing to say to the man.

However, he didn't resist. He wasn't under arrest, yet, he was merely answering some questions about this morning's events.

There was a crowd outside the hospital that hadn't been there when they'd gone in.

Local reporters had piled into the car park and were keen to ask questions. Gil ignored them. They all wanted to know what had happened to Jasmine, was it the River Man again? Was he real after the crew had called it a hoax?

How did they find out so much so fast?

One of Jasmine's crew—he could tell from the shirt she was wearing with the show logo on—pushed her way forward. 'I can't get any answers and this lot are vultures. Where are Luke and Calvin?'

'Luke was helping the police. We witnessed a suicide this morning.' That seemed like it had happened years ago, not this morning.

'I thought that was BS.' She put her hands on her hips.

Gil shook his head. 'Calvin was out at the ranger's station—the police brought the ranger in thinking he was the River Man.'

'Clearly that isn't the case. Is Jasmine okay?'

The cop coughed, clearly not impressed with the delay.

Gil ignored him. 'She will be ... they might let you wait with her.' Gil gave the woman a pointed look. 'We wouldn't want the River Man to strike again.'

Her lips twisted. 'Yeah. Got ya.' She turned and marched toward the doors.

The press moved closer, still asking questions.

This time when the cop suggested Gil get in the car, he did.

The drive to the station took longer than it should've because of the festival. People were having fun. Listening to the music, and buying local crafts, spending up at the local eateries. Bitterwood needed the festival, but they didn't need the darkness that it had sprung from. He had no idea how to keep them separate.

In the next breath, he realised it wasn't his problem.

He wasn't the mayor and he wasn't on the committee. He might be the chief's son, but it was well-known there was a rift.

Gil stared out the window. The town he'd grown up in wasn't the place he knew, and he wasn't sure it was the place he wanted to stay. The only place he wanted to be right now was with Jasmine.

*** 

Gil sat in the interview room, not sure if should get a lawyer before he started answering questions. They would want to know about Bert and about finding Jasmine. How much did he tell about the rest? At the moment it was the word of Theo Royle against his father. There was nothing concrete.

The door opened and his father walked in. 'You've had quite the day.'

'Yeah.' Not the one he'd planned, that was for sure.

His father sat. 'I know you heard some pretty wild accusations, and I can understand that in the heat of the moment that they might have seemed plausible, but *she's* safe and it's all okay.'

'Theo has been arrested then, for kidnapping her, hurting her?'

'We don't know what happened. We haven't spoken to her. I doubt her cousin would really hurt her. He was helping to look for her.' His father smiled.

Gil pressed his lips together. That was the line that was being fed to everyone. 'And the ranger, who had nothing to do with the deer deaths?'

'Um, he has been released. It was a misunderstanding.'

'Dad.' He looked his father in the eyes. 'You are so full of bullshit you don't know top from bottom. The secret is out. The reporter at the hospital had heard the gossip. Kind of strange that the woman who uncovered it was suddenly targeted? That the old man killed himself.' He'd never forget what Bert had said.

*Be a better man than your father.*

'You don't know what you're talking about.' But his father had paled.

'Yeah, I do. Bert didn't tell me what your role was, but you knew who killed the deer. Who killed that man twenty years ago and who abducted Jasmine. You've known all along.'

'It was the River Man.' His father stood. 'You can talk to one of the officers and give your statement. Cool your heels for a bit until you see sense. You've had a big day.'

Gil stood. 'This isn't the nineteen-hundreds. People aren't stupid. You can't shut down a whole TV show. They're going to talk about the hoax and people will speculate who it could have been. People in town are going to wonder who the killer is among them. They'll look at you and know you did nothing.'

His father stepped back. 'Shut your mouth.'

'No. I won't sit back and let the lies of a few create fear for many.'

There was a knock on the door, two seconds later the young cop stuck his head in. He glanced at the chief. How much he heard? It didn't matter, after today his father's career was over. 'Chief, what should I do with Luke Melrose? His lawyer is demanding that if he isn't being charged with anything, he be released.'

His father drew in a couple of breaths. It was all unravelling. There was a glimmer of fear in his father's eyes. Something he'd never seen before. 'Let him go. The sooner they're out of Bitterwood the better.'

Did his father really think that would be enough? That everyone would forget?

His father turned and his heel and strode out.

Eventually someone found the time to take Gil's statement about the suicide of Bert Royle and the rescue of Jasmine Heydon. Then he was free to go.

He made his way back across town to the hospital on foot. He stopped when he saw the *Cryptid or Hoax?* team all set up and recording near some of the festival signs. They were talking about the power of myths, and how even now the belief in them meant that every strange occurrence was blamed on something that couldn't be real. There was no mention that it was a hoax. Perhaps they weren't allowed.

Looking at Calvin as he talked, he seemed to be having the time of his life.

It was only when the camera stopped that the smile faded.

He beckoned Gil. 'Thank you.'

'It was nothing. I did what anyone would.'

'No you didn't. No one here would've helped her. In a big city you might be invisible but at least people aren't pretending that everything is peachy. Did the cops arrest him?'

'I don't think so.' Theo was still out there; would he try again? Surely he wouldn't keep on being the River Man?

'I think you'll find some cops are arriving from the city to help out. It's not going to look good for your father.'

'I know.' His father had always been happy to shrug and blame the River Man, and all those times he'd been right. It had been the River Man and his father had known who that was. The good Easton name was going to lose its polish and power.

His halo had well and truly been knocked off.

\*\*\*

When Jasmine woke up, there were people waiting to see her. Luke and Calvin, a cop—not Chief Easton, notably—a lawyer from the TV station and Gil. The doctor who was treating her had told her that she didn't have to see any of them if she didn't want to.

She didn't know what she wanted to do, but she needed to know what was going on. And what had happened while she was unconscious. She remembered the cold chewing through like a living thing intent on getting to the juicy warmth of her innards. She remembered Gil holding her and never wanting to leave his embrace.

The rest was kind of fuzzy.

Her mother was at her bedside holding her hand. 'I'll step out, call your father and make sure he's okay with the grandkids.'

Jasmine opened her mouth to argue that he'd be fine but shut it again. Her mother had left him with the grandkids. That was a big a step. So Jasmine just smiled and nodded.

The local cop and the big city lawyer came in and she gave her statement. It was clear that no one had arrested Theo. They thought he'd been trying to find her. And now she was neatly tucked into bed waiting for him to show up. She wasn't safe here. All she wanted to do was go home, home being Tricia's apartment.

She made it very clear that Theo had confessed to acting as the River Man, that he'd killed several times, and that he'd had special gloves and that was how he'd scratched her. 'Have you found the rental car?'

'It was on fire,' the cop confessed.

They all knew that meant there would be no evidence left.

'But I think I've got enough.' The cop stood.

'You'll be bringing Theo Royle in for questioning?' the lawyer asked, but it was more of an order.

The cop swallowed and nodded. 'Yes.'

If the chief did the questioning, then Theo would walk. They were in it together—parasite and host couldn't be separated, and they were so tightly enmeshed it was hard to tell which was which. The lawyer showed the cop out then turned back to her. 'You want to press charges against your cousin?'

All the times she'd been told about family loyalty rang in her head. What loyalty, they'd had none for her. 'Yes. They might be the only ones that stick.'

Her cousin had tried to kill her to protect his family's criminal activities. Activities that had put extra cash into the pocket of Chief Easton. And it had been going on for generations. Horse rustling had given way to a chop shop and then drugs, with the River Man creating enough fear or enough of a distraction that no one wanted to look too closely at what went on upstream. And most people believed the cops when they said everything was fine and they were taking care of things. What a scam. If Theo hadn't gotten a taste for blood, how long would it have continued?

'Internal review will enjoy digging around. I'm sure they'd find something of interest on the chief.'

She nodded.

Poor Gil. This was his father they were talking about bringing down, but she wasn't going to lie to protect him. However she understood now why Chief Easton had wanted her away from his son. When had the chief noticed he was in too deep?

Had it been after the first murder twenty years ago? Or earlier, when the secrets had been handed from father to son and the choices were remain silent or risk the family's reputation?

They'd probably never know.

She didn't want to know. That was one mystery she was happy to let someone else work on. She'd uncovered the hoax of the River Man and that was more than enough for her.

'Can you send Gil in?'

The lawyer nodded and stepped out. Less than a minute later, Gil was in the doorway. He looked tired. The bottom of his jeans were muddy, as though he hadn't been home since putting her in the boat.

Her eyes brimmed with tears.

She could've died on that riverbank.

# Chapter 14

Gil watched as Jasmine folded her feet up on his sofa. She'd been released from hospital that morning and was leaving tomorrow. The TV show had a schedule, and if the episode on the River Man wasn't approved for airing, they'd have to come up with another one to fill in. Jasmine had suggested a more general look at amphibious humanoids. It could be called a special.

He handed her a cup of coffee and sat in the armchair opposite her. The bandage on her arm was clearly visible. She had stitches in her leg and arm and would probably have scars.

This whole thing was going to leave scars on the town and both families.

'I am sorry about your father.'

Gil grimaced. No one could've predicted that his father was in on the River Man scam and taking a share from the Royle-run chop shop. Apparently Theo had started talking before he'd even been put in the cop car, and the gossip had travelled just as fast. Gil's father had vanished, unwilling to face the consequences.

That left Gil and his mother to bear the brunt of the looks. There were already looks. Some people were still blaming Jasmine for coming in and poking around.

'All his talk about doing the right thing and being part of the town, and having the right social circle, it was all lies.' That was the hardest bit to swallow. His father had been a cop, a trusted member of the community and he'd used that to his advantage.

'He wanted you to have the life he couldn't. We don't know what happened between Bert and him. Maybe there were threats?' She cradled the cup as though she was still cold.

Yesterday he thought he was going to lose her. Tomorrow he would. His chest hadn't stopped aching. This wasn't the lightweight lust of a sixteen-year-old, this was love. He couldn't tell her because she had a life somewhere else. He'd known she wouldn't stay, but he'd jumped in anyway.

'You don't have to defend him.' He wasn't going to waste his time defending his father, but he had to be there for his mother.

Jasmine was quiet for a moment, studying her coffee. 'I wish I had longer here.'

He smiled. 'So do I.'

'Really?' She'd come around to see him when she could've just called to say goodbye and stayed at the motel. She didn't have to be here. But she wanted to be here. With him. She glanced up and her lips curved. 'Maybe without all the drama.'

'Like, for a visit?' He didn't want to be getting all his hopes up. 'Or did you want to do the long-distance dating thing.'

She nodded. 'Both. I realise that will totally scandalise some people, and I know you're the one who has to live here with all the gossip.' Her words were getting faster as though she was trying to talk him out of agreeing.

'We can make it work.' This was the push he needed to get off his butt and get a qualification. He'd fallen into his job of running the store, and while that might be enough here, it wouldn't be enough in Seattle. The idea of leaving Bitterwood had taken on a shine it had never had before. There was a whole world out there that didn't even know Bitterwood existed.

She got up and walked over; she hesitated for a moment and then sat on his lap. 'I'm not going to say goodbye.'

He put his arms around her and pulled her close. She was still holding the coffee cup, so he took it out of her hands and put it on the little table next to the armchair where his grandfather had kept his book and his glasses. He held her hands, so glad they were warm in his. She wasn't leaving before he'd told her how he felt. 'I love you.'

She gasped and her eyes went wide. 'You don't have to—'

'Yes I do. After yesterday I can't pretend that I don't care. This isn't a rewarming of old coals. I want to keep seeing you, even if it is whenever you can fit me in.'

'I want to be with you. I'll be back more often than once every ten years, Gil. I can come back every few weeks.

You could come and see me sometimes.'

'I plan to.' He wasn't going to sit back and wait for life to happen or to knock on his door. It had knocked and brought Jasmine back into his life. Only a fool would close the door on a second chance like that.

'Good.' She kissed him. 'I still have a few hours before I have to pack up.'

'Are you sure?' He didn't want her tearing her stitches.

She nodded. 'I want to make sure that you think of me every time you go to bed, the way I will be thinking of you. I never stopped thinking of you.' Another kiss, slower deeper. 'This time I know I love you.'

His heart gave a little jump. He stood, scooping her up and carried to her his bedroom. Every second was precious when she would be darting in and out of his life. 'Let's not waste the time you have left here.'

She laughed as she landed on his bed and drew him close. 'I'm going to miss you.'

'I'll miss you too. But I'll be waiting.'

'I'll be counting the days until I come back,' she said.

So would he.

# Bestselling Titles by Escape Publishing...

Thanks for reading *Close to the Truth.* I hope you enjoyed it.

If you liked this book, here are my other titles, **Diving into Trouble, In the Spotlight, Out of Rhythm, Out of Place, Out of Time, Out of Chances,** *Secret Confessions: Backstage – Kelly,* **Secret Confessions: Sydney Housewives – Meagan.**

Sign up to our newsletter romance.com.au/newsletter/and find out about new releases, must-read series and **ebook deals** at romance.com.au.

Reviews can help readers find books, and I am grateful for all honest reviews. Thank you for taking the time to let others know what you've read, and what you thought.

**Share your reading experience on:**

**Facebook**

Instagram

romance.com.au

Discover another great read from Escape Publishing...

**Diving into Trouble**
**Shona Husk**

*A submarine, a one-night-stand, and a forbidden workplace romance...*

Kurt Garland is at a crossroads: sign for another two years as a submariner or leave and rejoin civilian life. With only weeks to make up his mind, he's torn between the financial stability and mateship of life in the Navy, and the freedom and balance outside of the military. With big life decisions on the line, Kurt needs space to think, so a one-night-stand with a sexy stranger is all he can commit to. Until his sexy stranger shows up on his submarine...

Getting accepted into the Submarine Corps was an enormous career goal for

Rainy Miller, and she has no intention of screwing it up. A Marine Technician for the last eight years in the surface fleet, Rainy craves the new challenges of a submariner. With her training complete, she's about to join a boat for the first time, and her career relies on a good impression. When her one-night-stand shows up in the galley, she has to shut it down, walk away, pretend it never happened. But all submariners know that secrets don't stay secret for long on a sub.

Find it *here.*

# In the Spotlight
## Shona Husk

*A diva who lives for the spotlight, a sailor deeply in the closet, a love that will change them both*

Ripley Malone is returning to Perth in triumph. A principal ballet dancer in a production that has critics raving, he is an unqualified success, and all the small-minded people that made his life hell can kiss his lycra-covered ass. But behind the make-up and the glitter and the costumes, Ripley is beginning to tire, tire of the competition, the drive, the endless parade of meaningless lovers.

For Pierce Lovell, joining the Navy was a way out of rural Victoria, but becoming a submariner comes with its own set of challenges. The close living quarters and long months away are awkward enough without adding any extra tension around his sexuality. The fear is probably in his head, but he isn't taking any chances with his career. He gets by on anonymous one-night-stands every time they come to shore and keeps his heart well-shielded. But one night with Ripley opens the tantalising possibility of more.

Through a mistake Ripley is injured. He can't dance. His wings are clipped and he crashes down and hits the earth hard. Pierce knows their affair can't possibly end in anything but heartache, but he can't stay away. As Ripley heals and reassesses his life, he is determined not to make the same mistakes again. That means letting someone see the vulnerable side of him. But vulnerability for Pierce could cost him everything.

Find it *here.*

Lightning Source UK Ltd.
Milton Keynes UK
UKHW020637060223
416537UK00012B/2592